Changing Tides

The Sirenia Chronicles Book I

Kristen Braddock

Changing Tides

Sirenia Chronicles: Book One
ISBN: 978-1-7371027-1-7

Copyright© 2021 by Kristen Braddock
www.kristenbraddock.com

This is a work of fiction. Any resemblance to actual persons, places, or events is purely coincidental.

Cover Design by Miblart

Front matter character art by Ari Brodeur

Book Interior by Kristen Braddock

For every person who pretended to be a mermaid in the pool.

colored hair
internal gills via eustachian tube
wrap top made of kelp
pelvic fins
caudal fin

ONE

I winced as the front door slammed shut behind me. "My bad!"

"Willemina Anne Farraige! How many times do I have to tell you to be careful? The wind's too strong this time of day."

I winced at her use of my full name. I had gone by Billie since I was a kid.

My aunt rounded the corner, lips pressed tightly together, but within moments, a smile spread back across her face. Her brown eyes sparkled with flecks of gold the way my mother's used to when she flashed a grin. A trait passed onto me as well.

My breath hitched as it did every time Aunt Joan reminded me of my mother. The pain from the loss came in waves, but it had gotten easier. I gave an apologetic smile as I tried to ignore the distracting ache in my chest.

My aunt wasn't the family type. She was the type of person others called a free spirit. Her wanderlust was strong, and it often took her to the far corners of the world. But four years ago, she ceased her life of frivolous meandering, choosing instead to take care of me.

It was nice and all, but we never became too close. In the end, I couldn't replace the sister she lost, and she couldn't replace my mother. We were a stark reminder to each other of what we had lost, and despite the love we clearly had for one another, we kept our distance. I'll admit it was my fault; I pulled away more, and I hated myself for it. But I was scared that if I moved on, if I loved her the way I loved my parents, I would replace them.

After graduating from high school a year ago, I tried to convince her to get on with her life, but she kept repeating the same mantra she had been reciting since she first arrived, "You come first."

"Lord, look at your hair!" Aunt Joan swept her hand across the knotted mess atop my head. "Did you even tie it back while you were at the beach?"

I brushed her hand away. "Of course not." It was constraining to keep the breeze from flowing through my hair. The breeze brought the ocean to me.

Moving farther into the hallway, a medley of tomatoes, garlic, and wine wafting from the kitchen took over my senses.

Aunt Joan smiled. "Chicken parmesan. The best recipe I picked up in Sicily! Your mother's favorite."

Her concerned look made my insides twist. We both stood there staring at one another until my eyes dropped.

"I'm so sorry, sweetie. I wasn't thinking." She trailed off, wringing her hands together.

I tore my eyes away from Aunt Joan's worried look and headed for the kitchen. I adored my aunt, but didn't want her constant concern and pity.

I picked at my nails and frowned. My parents had died, and it was terrible, but I wasn't some china doll that needed careful handling, as though I'd break at any minute.

When I entered the kitchen, a disastrous sight welcomed me. There were at least ten dirty plates stacked in the middle of the marble island and dirty knives of varying sizes strewn about. Uncooked pasta layered across the counter, some their full length, while other pieces were so broken, they were close to becoming sand. I glared at the pieces of smashed tomato on the floor.

The mess was worse than usual, but this was my typical aunt, a bit of a whirlwind, which was fun when she'd visit as a kid, but had been difficult to live with. She had never wanted kids, and she tried her best, which I was grateful for, but it was a stark contrast to the clean kitchen I had grown up with.

"What the—" I trailed off.

"You know I'm not a tidy cook, just a good one," Aunt Joan said as she blew a black curl out of her face.

It was true; my aunt was a wonderful cook. After one semester in college, she had dropped out, choosing to travel the world and learn to cook foods from nearly every continent—tracing their origins and learning from the locals. She was fearless and welcomed new challenges. So different from me.

"Go upstairs and take a shower while I finish." Aunt Joan ushered me out of the kitchen.

A step squeaked beneath me as I climbed the wooden staircase. My gaze stayed on my turquoise-painted toenails to avoid the smiling photos that hung on the wall. Smiles I hadn't seen in six years.

The stairs ended at a short hall, two bedrooms on the right, and a bathroom and master bedroom on the left. My aunt and I both lived on the right, neither of us willing to take my parents' suite despite it having its own bathroom.

I opened the last door on the right, flung my black backpack onto my sea-foam comforter, and hit play on my CD player. Tony Bennett's blues filled the air. The CD player had been my father's—a black, nineties Magnavox. It was one of my most prized possessions, along with my parents' CD collection which was a mix of classic rock and blues. I didn't care how outdated it was, I would cherish it forever.

When I was younger, my mom would make breakfast for me in the morning, blasting music as she cooked. We would dance around the kitchen, and she'd flip a pancake in the pan, typically causing half of it to end up on the floor. We'd laugh, and my mother would say, "I always liked them crescent-shaped anyway."

I loved music almost as much as I loved the ocean.

The marine world was another hobby my parents got me into, which was not surprising considering they both worked for the Fisheries Department. I loved the endless possibilities, how the sea was the last frontier on land to still be discovered. I loved how fish were curious and would swim right up to my face. I had tried to explain to land-lovers that I had never been on a hike and had an array of squirrels rush me or had a staring contest with a deer or fox. But in the ocean, it was different. I'd been bumped by turtles, surrounded by schools of fish, and inspected by sharks. It was exhilarating in a way I never experienced on land, and I never knew what would happen next. Having had a family to introduce me to this magnificent world was something I would never take for granted.

A pit formed in my stomach as I stared at a picture of my parents in their mid-twenties graduating together.

Shaking my head to clear it, I grabbed my towel, and headed for the bathroom. A quick ten minutes was all I needed, and I was clean and in a fresh pair of leggings and a loose T-shirt.

"Dinner's ready!" Aunt Joan hollered from downstairs.

I pulled the towel off my head and ran my fingers through my loose curls as I walked down the creaking steps. Distracted, my foot missed a step, and I plunged forward. I grasped for the banister to stop myself from tumbling down, and a searing ache shot through my hand as my palm slammed into the wood.

Crap. That was going to leave a bruise.

I continued down the stairs, more wary this time, and then entered the kitchen, massaging my palm and plopping down on a stool at the kitchen island.

"How was your day? Did you meet anyone?" Aunt Joan always asked the same questions. She never seemed to lose hope that I would return to the normalcy of my previous life: hanging out with friends, getting good grades, or rejoining the swim team.

"I saw some frigate birds. The male's red chest was all puffed up trying to get some ladies," I joked before shoving a fork full of chicken and pasta into my mouth. My taste buds exploded, per usual with Aunt Joan's cooking.

Aunt Joan pouted. "I was hoping for something juicy. Maybe a cute guy talked to you or something."

I grimaced. "Boys have cooties. No thanks."

"What are you, eight?" Aunt Joan laughed.

"No, but most boys seem to be eight. Mom always said men were useless between the ages of eighteen and twenty-four, and I'm beginning to think she was right."

"They can't be that bad," Aunt Joan insisted, and I returned a blank stare. "Okay, well, one can hope."

I had yet to meet anyone to prove otherwise. The guys in my circle were too immature, and the girls were insecure. Plus, my social life was as shallow as a tide pool, aka non-existent, which wasn't inspiring for my love life.

I stifled a laugh. Every once in a while, we had these easy moments, where we didn't walk on eggshells and could mention my mom. They were nice, and I wished we could have more of them. It had been four years, but it was still so awkward for us. It sucked. Living in this house was like being haunted by them at times.

"How're classes going? Find anything you're interested in pursuing?"

I answered with a nonchalant shrug before gobbling another bite of pasta.

"I know you've said no in the past, but I really think a meeting with your parents' old boss could help with some brainstorming for your future," my aunt said with an encouraging smile. "You know, it took me a while to find what I loved, but I had to go out into the world and try new things to find it."

I pushed the noodles around on my plate. "I guess it couldn't hurt."

Aunt Joan clapped with enthusiasm. "Great! I'll email him tomorrow to set up a meeting!"

I gave a closed-lip smile. Aunt Joan had done so much for me, and I had spent the last year flopping around aimlessly like a fish out of water. It was the least I could do.

I peeked over at a papier-mâché dolphin hanging on the wall that I had made in an art class I took last year.

Aunt Joan's eyebrows knitted together. "Sweetie, this'll be good. Going in the ocean every day and listening to music are not the only things in life."

I gave her a doubtful look. "You forgot eating."

Aunt Joan leveled me with a glare. "Keep it up and it'll be Hot Pockets for a month."

"Guess I'll have to use the amazing cooking skills my aunt taught me to make my own food." I grinned at her.

Aunt Joan winked, and I smiled because it was clear she knew I was buttering her up. "Well, I'm glad I could give you something."

"You give me a lot," I said. We shifted in our seats, looking away from one another. Great, back to our usual avoidant behavior. The need to lighten the mood and make it less awkward pulled at my mouth. "Like cell phones," I added with a chuckle.

Aunt Joan threw her napkin at me. "Christmas was the last time! I'm not going to buy you another one just because sand gets into it or it gets wet…again."

I pouted briefly before giving her a sly grin. I went through a phone about every six months because of mishaps at the beach and often had used an Android phone without data. My newest device was an iPhone, a gift from my aunt; it was the first time I had owned a brand new phone.

My finger slid along the plate, scooping up any remnants of sauce I could devour.

Aunt Joan shook her head at my habit, but mirth glistened in her eyes.

I popped my tomato-free finger out of my mouth with a grin.

"Come on, time to do dishes," my aunt said with an eye roll.

Smirking, I rose from the table, picking up our plates on the way to the sink.

Whoever doesn't cook, cleans. Sadly, this meant I had cleaning duty most nights, but it was worth it for these savory dishes.

I coughed, catching Aunt Joan's attention, and pointed at an ad I had printed for a rental space in the main area of town.

"Not this again," she groaned, putting her head on the table.

I suppressed a snicker. Who was the actual child in this relationship?

Aunt Joan raised her head. "I know you want me to open a restaurant, but it's too risky. I don't have the finances for it."

I raised an eyebrow. "Like hell you don't."

"Language," Aunt Joan warned. "I'm not using the money your parents left you. That was to ensure you were well taken care of. They wanted college covered and a roof over your head." Crossing her arms, she leaned back in her chair, waiting for my retort.

I had nothing. Their will had been very specific—funds were set aside to cover college, even a Master's degree. The house had been put in my name and paid in full. There was no mortgage and university money couldn't be diverted, which meant the only thing I could do for additional money was take out a mortgage on the house. Aunt Joan wouldn't let me.

I sighed, knowing any response I could give her wouldn't go anywhere, and I wasn't about to disobey the last request from my parents.

Placing the last dish on the drying rack, I strode over to Aunt Joan and gave her a small hug. "Thanks for the food."

"Goodnight, sweetie." Aunt Joan stroked my hair. "Have fun working on physics. Although, how you learn that online, I have no idea."

"Night," I said and headed upstairs.

Ψ

"When you go out at night, just a few days after the full moon, there are these teeny tiny, little crustaceans that will spit out this fluid…" My mother was holding up her fingers, as if showing the size of an animal that you could barely see with the naked eye.

"Ew, that sounds gross!" I stuck my tongue out with down-turned lips and squinty eyes. "Blech!"

"No!" My father intervened, "The fluids would light up! Swirling up to the surface."

I widened my eyes as I watched as my dad swirled his finger toward the ceiling.

"The light of the fluid was bluish white. You shine your flashlight through the water, and there would be thousands of bright swirls all around you! It was like you were flying through the stars." My mom beamed down at me.

"You and dad flew in the stars?" I breathed out as sleep pulled at my eyelids.

"The swirls looked like magic." My father bent down and kissed my forehead, pulling the sea-foam comforter closer to my chin.

"Wow," I said.

"Good night, sweet girl. Dream among the stars of the ocean." My mom gave me a kiss before turning off the bedside lamp.

I blinked open my eyes to an empty room streaked with rays of the morning sun. My head swam with my parents' faces and an ache formed in my chest.

Rolling over, I pushed my face into the pillow, smothering

myself and the dream. Memories that came as dreams were like an attack on my mind, ripping me away from reality, then plunging me back in. They were the worst. What was even harder was how real they felt, like I had gone back in time. I had them a ton when my parents first passed. Now, I could go months without one—which only made it more jarring when they did occur.

A tear pricked at my eye, and I swiped it away in annoyance.

I would not cry. I had spilled enough tears and needed to move on with my life. The ocean would help clear my head.

I dragged myself out of bed, snagging my bathing suit off the back of my desk chair, and snuck down the stairs to the front door. I grabbed my snorkel, mask, and fins, which I had left hanging on the coat rack, and left the quiet house.

Outside, I tasted the salty air on the tip of my tongue. The beach breeze whipped my sleep-tangled hair across my face. I pulled the knotted mess into a quick bun as I ran down the sidewalk. My sandals clacked against the quiet morning, like a crowing rooster waking up the world. A wave of bubbling euphoria shot through my limbs like a belly drop on a roller coaster.

Soon, the rumbling of waves grew louder. My heart rate picked up, and the corners of my mouth turned upright. Sliding off my brown sandals and slipping them onto my fingers, I dug my feet into the cool sand. It was still too early for the sand to be hot from the beating sun.

The seagulls squawked good morning and eyeballed the sandals in my hand, probably hoping for fries or a hot dog.

I yearned for the ocean, my personal siren, and my skin tingled with anticipation. My calves burned from the uneven, sandy ground as I ran with grains of sand flinging from my feet.

Nearing the foamy ocean, I relished the sound of the waves. Nothing could replicate its authenticity. This was home.

I threw my gear into a pile and stripped down to my green swimsuit. I picked up my mask with the snorkel already attached and slipped it over my head until it rested around my neck.

My parents had drilled into me throughout my childhood: *Never put the mask on your forehead, because that means that you're in trouble.* It was SCUBA diving 101, something everyone was trained to know—if someone is panicking in the water, they tend to become more careless with their expensive gear and a wave could swipe the mask off their head—if only such a thing could have helped them.

I winced, pushing the reminder of my parents from my mind. I would start the day off right, not dwelling on their deaths.

I scanned the beach, seeing only people out for their morning runs. Holding my fins, I bounded down the sandy bank to the warm Floridian water.

The ocean retracted as I ran toward it—as though we were playing tag—until a crashing wave thrust the tepid water just below my knees.

I placed the mask over my eyes and nose, and my lips surrounded the mouthpiece on the snorkel. I took a deep breath, filled my lungs with fresh air, and plunged into the open blue.

TWO

A giddy smile crossed my lips, and water seeped into my mouth from around the snorkel. Unfazed, I blew hard into the mouthpiece with the leftover air in my lungs. The water burst from the top, clearing the airway.

Dozens of fish flitted around me.

Surgeonfish, damselfish, parrotfish, butterflyfish, I quizzed myself on the different species.

Moving farther away from shore, I watched the sandy bottom fall away. Thankfully, the visibility didn't falter, and I could still easily see seventy feet in front of me.

I floated atop the water, belly down, letting the waves lift and support me. This was the life right here—warm water, animal encounters, and a place to clear my mind. Nothing could beat it.

My hands interlocked in an arc over my head, as I rested in the water. A sunken car tire beneath me called to me to check it out. The amount of junk that ended up in the ocean was getting ridiculous. But then, most people couldn't see the harm they inadvertently caused to the creatures that lived under the sea. In the end, we were land animals. Chopping down the rainforest or burning mountains? Sure, we see the damage and try to put an end to it. But heaven forbid we try to protect what covers 70 percent of our planet.

Sometimes it was hard to stay positive, to keep trying, to come here day after day and pick up trash. But the alternative was worse, and I couldn't live with myself if I gave up. Thankfully, the ocean did a good job in repurposing things into homes for animals. And I definitely wanted to see what was around that tire.

I breathed slow and deep—in, out, in, out, in. On the last breath, I filled my lungs to maximum capacity and thrust my hands downward, using my upper body to dip below the surface.

Once my fins reached the water line, I took long, measured kicks. Staying calm and focused, I quickly reached the ocean floor.

Inches from touching the sandy bottom, I oriented my body until I was hovering parallel with the sand. Little crabs scurried along the bottom, dipping into holes in the sand which were their homes. Goat fish with whiskers on their chin trifled through the bottom, creating plumes of dust around them as they searched for food. Tunnels littered the ground with who-knows-what inside each tiny hole. It was magical to see these tiny worlds, tiny creatures, and mosey alongside them like I belonged there too.

The tire had algae and new coral lining the sides. Coral grew inches, at best, each year, so they were small, but new ecosystems had to start somehow. I peeked inside the lip of the circular rubber, hoping something interesting would be hiding inside, but to my disappointment, there was nothing.

Swimming along, I repressed my smile so my mask wouldn't fill with water. But I loved how none of the fish in the ocean feared me. It was an unconventional trust not known on land. In the ocean, I was in an aquarium with life all around me.

Two minutes passed, and my lungs ached from the carbon dioxide build up. I shifted toward the surface, kicking my fins harder with each second that passed.

A few feet from the surface, I exhaled, watching the horde of bubbles race me to the top of the water.

My lungs were tight from the lack of air. I had lost track of time on the free dive, and they now felt like a squeezed sponge. Breaking the surface, I inhaled a lungful of fresh air, followed by three controlled breaths before returning my face to the water.

If I wasn't careful with my breathing technique, I could have a shallow water blackout. This was the exact reason I had promised my parents to never free dive alone, and why they had forced me to take a class and get certified. But they were gone, and I had no other ocean lovers in my life. So I had no other choice.

Even as I caught my breath, my heart beat fast—I'd definitely cut it too close. My parents would have reamed me for a dive like that, especially without a buddy present to help me if I passed out.

Whoopsies.

I cross my heart I won't push my limits like that again. Well, at least, not today.

I continued to snorkel along the top of the water, inspecting the animals' behaviors as I went. It was nerdy, I know. But to me it was more than 'oo, look at the pretty fish'.

Two wrasses swirled around one another before shooting higher into the water—a part of their mating dance. I noticed a symbiotic relationship—a red and white striped cleaner shrimp hopped into the gaping mouth of a casually floating snapper. The shrimp got to eat, and the snapper got a marine dentist.

My aunt was right; I really should meet with my parents' boss. I had avoided my future long enough, but the thrill I got from watching what most people would consider mundane proved I could enjoy doing this for the rest of my life. It wasn't just the fish that fascinated me. The physics of the waves, the circular motion of each water molecule as it moved around my body and slowly drifted west with the current—I loved every aspect of this world.

Maybe I'd become a teacher or use research as a way to travel the world like Aunt Joan. I could dive in every ocean and sea that exists on Earth.

I chuckled to myself at the thought. But it was something, wasn't it?

The problem was, as much as I loved the ocean, it was the thing that took my parents away from me. Here I was, floating around admiring the beauty and feeling energized by the thing that murdered my parents. Yes, I had been raised this way. Yes, it was my connection to them as well. But any sane person would have hated it the moment it happened. Car crash victims tend to avoid cars for a while. What did I do? The next day I came and sat at the beach. I freakin' came to the beach and felt calmer! What kind of sick and twisted individual loved the thing that left them an orphan?

Apparently, this demented human being right here.

With another deep inhale, I refocused. I came here to clear my mind of my parents, of my dream, and the opposite was happening. I don't know why they were on my mind more than usual, but I didn't need the distraction. Distractions caused accidents, and accidents caused deaths.

Diving again, I pushed away my distractions to focus on the present. I equalized the pressure in my ears as I swam through the water column towards the ocean floor. Within seconds, I was twenty feet down, and picking up scraps of trash along the bottom. Boats commonly anchored off these shores, and it was common to find bundles of trash that had fallen off the bow of the boat.

More plastic. Just what the ocean needs, something else for an animal to consume and probably die from.

I could become an ocean conservationist. Although, I'd heard that working for nonprofits was less about spreading awareness and more about writing grants to stay funded. What a buzzkill. Why couldn't humans make better decisions? It's not like other options aren't available. We could use bamboo toothbrushes instead of plastic, reusable bottles or bags, switch to solar, and so many other things that could make a huge difference!

A plastic bag drifted along the bottom like a tumbleweed. I quickly caught it before it could wrap around a coral head.

Thirty feet to my right, a midnight parrotfish swam next to a rusty hunk of metal. My heart raced with excitement.

I hadn't seen a midnight parrotfish in over a year!

The fish was about a foot and a half long with an upper lip that looked as though it had enhancement surgery. It was a midnight blue with black streaks along the scales on the side. Baby blue splotches decorated the fish's face.

Midnight parrotfish had been my father's favorite fish. When I was younger, we'd have competitions each year to see who could spot the most midnight parrotfish. At the end of the year, the winner would get a prize. I won every time. I'm 99 percent sure my father let me win though. But with the prize being a chocolate shake and a new CD, there was no way I would call him out on it.

Adrenaline raced through my veins, and my eyes scanned the surface. I didn't want to push myself like I had earlier. But there was time—I could make it back safely.

I had started freediving at twelve and had practiced holding my breath so I could last longer underwater. I had no interest in becoming a professional, I just loved being able to spend as much time as possible immersing myself in the sea. The longest I had ever held my breath was three minutes and twenty-three seconds, but that was without any movement.

The shimmering blue scales flashed again.

I squinted to see the dark blue tail flopping from side to side. Contorting my body to get a better look at it, my feet reached for the sky, and the corals hung above my head. I pushed aside a metal wire pressing against my face as I held onto a rusted opening on the side of metal contraption that had been warped with time. I peered at the parrotfish, as it munched on the damselfish's algal gardens growing on the old hunk of metal. It never ceased to amaze me that nature always finds a way to take back its own—junk turned into a garden of food.

Each crunch reverberated and enveloped around me underwater. The noises consumed me without a need for earphones. The water was like its own booming sound system, with every organism being one of the many instruments in a gigantic orchestra.

The parrotfish noticed me watching, and froze. Both of us stilled while we surveyed each other.

A few moments passed, and my lungs pulled tight. It was time to leave.

With a mental sigh, I pressed away from the gap in the metal, and flipped myself back over to begin my ascent. I rose slightly, but when I kicked with my right foot, I felt a tug.

A wire encircled my ankle.

I reached down for the strap on my left calf for my emergency knife. I carried one for times like these. Not for use as a weapon, but in case of entanglement.

My hand fumbled for a moment, grasping nothing but the skin of my thigh. My heart hiccupped.

I had forgotten my knife!

Little oxygen remained in my lungs; still, I swooshed over to my right ankle to undo the wire. My goggles fogged up. I couldn't see. I couldn't unwind the biting metal. Water leaked into the bottom of my mask, plugging my nose. My heart sped up, and I struggled to keep my mind calm.

It was no use. Freeing myself was futile.

Each second was agonizing. My lungs squeezed in my chest.

I tried to swim up again. Maybe I could pull it up with me.

The metal contraption wouldn't budge.

My fingers dug into my chest as panic seized my muscles. My burning lungs screamed for air. I couldn't breathe. I needed to breathe. Oh god, I was stuck. I was going to die. Wasn't drowning supposed to be peaceful? This was anything but that.

Tears mixed with the ocean water inside my mask.

I couldn't breathe. I couldn't see. I couldn't swim. I was stuck. And just like that, all I wanted to do was live. I had barely lived. I should've made a better effort with my aunt. I should've traveled or gone off to college. I should've tried dating like Aunt Joan suggested. I had no one, and I was going to die alone.

All the fish vanished, fleeing from my flailing limbs.

I needed to get to the surface. Dear God, please don't let me die this way.

My chest contracted in agony, begging for release and fresh air. My throat cinched together, constricting until tears of pain and fear puddled in my mask. I wanted to scream, to call for help. But there was nothing I could do.

I was trapped.

18

THREE

I t was forty seconds longer than I had ever held my breath.
Forty-one seconds.
Forty-two seconds.
Out of the corner of my blurry mask, a dark figure swam by.
Someone had seen me! Relief blossomed inside my aching chest.

Euphoria was beginning to set in from the lack of oxygen, and my body swayed side to side. The throb in my chest eased as a light tingling sensation spread through my limbs.

One minute and six seconds.

One minute and seven seconds.

Where were they? They'd better hurry the hell up or I was going to pass out soon.

The silhouette came closer. A swaying of what I assumed was hair. I was entranced by the aquamarine color of it blending into the ocean behind them. There was a blur of a huge fish behind the person.

One minute, twenty-two seconds.

I laughed out a few bubbles of air. I couldn't identify the species. My mind was playing tricks on me from the lack of oxygen.

They stopped inches from me.

I grasped their arm, emphasizing my need for help.

Help me, I screamed in my mind.

The blob reached out to steady me.

Giant blobfish! The last of my air escaped at the random and silly thought.

The person bent over, and I felt the tug of my leg.

Something smooth and scaly swiped against my cheek.

My vision darkened. Wait, no, my eyes were closed.

I pried them back open to see the person in front of me again.

They shook my shoulders and leaned toward me.

A wave of calm spread through my body. My muscles eased. My lungs didn't hurt anymore. It was almost over.

Their lips touched mine.

I opened my mouth, ready for the lungful of air they'd breathe in. I had never been so wrong.

The person blew water and spit into me, filling my mouth, filling my lungs.

My eyes widened in shock.

It burned. It felt like acid searing through me.

My left hand clawed my chest like I could rip it apart for the water to escape. The pain seared up my throat and into my head until it throbbed.

I screamed in agony, choking on the water and convulsing in place.

The commotion wrenched off my fins, mask, and snorkel. My ears sizzled away to my brain and sinuses. My legs felt lacerated. Every part of me was on fire despite the water surrounding me.

What in the world had she done? I didn't want to die, but I couldn't endure another second of this. I hoped I'd pass out soon enough.

I can't take this any longer. I'll end this myself—stop this on my own terms.

I took a deep breath through my nose, allowing additional water to rush in and knock me senseless.

Instead, my lungs receded, the burning stopped, and my body vibrated with new life. There was no more pain.

Then everything went dark.

The world was still black, but slowly the familiar crackles of the ocean pushed into my consciousness.

My lungs inflated with a deep breath.

Ah, sweet, sweet air.

I took another sip through my nose. A relieved sigh escaped me, and my body filled with satisfaction.

Opening my eyes, I blinked. Why were my snorkel and mask on the ground ten feet away? My hand flew to pick them up, but I stopped short. What the hell? How could I see so clearly? Wait. I was breathing…underwater! My hand flew to my mouth with a gasp.

"Are you okay?" A blue-haired woman about the same age as me, floated in front of me, smiling. Her eyes were wide and dark, a shade of deep violet. And her tail…her tail? The girl had a tail!

It was a pastel-green fish tail. The scales tapered off where her hips met her lower midriff. The filamentous fin was nearly translucent, maintaining a light green hue. At the end of the caudal fin, along with the pelvic fins, was a billowing membrane similar to that of a betta fish. There was strength in each muscular stroke of her tail.

"I can't believe it worked," she whispered to no one in particular. Her voice underwater was as clear as it would have been on land. Not warbled like a normal voice should be under the water.

I raised an inquisitive eyebrow.

The ocean moved gently across my skin with the current. Everything felt so real.

The pain was so great, surely I must have died. Or maybe I had passed out. Or perhaps—

"You transformed," the mermaid explained.

I shook my head to clear it. This didn't make any sense.

The mermaid's eyes skimmed down my body.

I followed her attentive gaze until it landed on a tail, one attached to the lower half of my body.

Transformed.

I squeaked in surprise and reached down to run my hands over the scales that matched the pattern of a midnight parrotfish.

Scales in varying blues highlighted with black shimmered in the water as I floated. They were hard like rocks, but smooth like the inside of a shell. I pushed down on the flesh, feeling the solid muscle where my legs should have been.

"Holy shit!" I screamed, scaring away the nearby fish.

The mermaid reached a hand out to me.

I flinched. There was no way this girl was touching me again.

"This can't be real," I breathed. I needed to get away, or wake up, or whatever the heck was going on—it needed to stop!

I tried to kick. My body didn't go anywhere. Instead, it twisted from side to side. A jolt of fear ran through me.

I didn't have legs, but I had a tail!

How many times had I played mermaid in the pool as a child? I could do this. I took off.

"Wait!" the girl hollered after me.

My instincts took over, and I swam faster than ever before. The tail was bound to me, and it didn't feel unnatural. My movement was similar to that of a dolphin. My muscles coursed and flexed with every movement, rolling down my body like a swell moving through the ocean.

The water streamed along my tail.

My pace slowed as my nerves settled. I peered over my shoulder, but the mermaid hadn't followed me. My mind twisted, still in shock with everything that had happened.

I had spent years learning about the ocean from scientists. There wasn't even a possible inkling of mermaids' existence. Granted, we had explored less than 10 percent of the ocean, but we had mapped the bottom. Even animals we rarely found alive, like the giant squid, left remnants along coastlines or floated dead on the surface. Even if they managed to stay hidden, there's no way there would be zero evidence of their existence…right?

My chest seized momentarily, and I slowed my pace further. The familiar pain caused a sensory memory from the first six months after my parents had died. My jaw locked and throat cinched as the need for silence bloomed in my chest. I was overwhelmed and my body wanted to protect me, urging me to become mute like it had once before.

I winced, forcing those dark times from my mind. If only it were that easy. I couldn't repress them. My recurring nightmares of drowning had returned. I'd had them for months on end. It took hours of therapy to work through them until I didn't have them anymore.

That must be what was happening now. Last night I dwelled on my parents more than I usually do. I reminisced too much and now I was having those nightmares again. Granted, in all previous situations I had woken up after blacking out. But a bad dream was definitely more logical than the fact I was a mermaid. That settled it. Definitely dreaming.

Snapping out of my mental loop, I scoured my surroundings for the first time. Nothing looked familiar. Only open water surrounded me.

Crap, lost at sea wasn't good in real life or a dream.

At the speed I was going, I could be anywhere. Below me, the depth of the ocean turned into a deep blue. And I could see the surface about thirty feet above me.

My SCUBA diver training kicked in—if you get lost, you need to surface to reorient yourself—so I swam toward the light.

The sun warmed my bronzed skin when my head popped out of the water. A smile stretched across my lips when I was able to take a breath of fresh air. Every sparkle on the surface of the water seemed bluer, and yet I could peer into the depths of the water like I wore special sunglasses to help refract the light. I didn't, and yet everything was so clear. Somehow sounds were louder, too, like I could hear every wave move closer to shore, and the wind whipping across the surface like running mallets along a xylophone.

Thank the heavens.

Resting at the trough between the swells of waves, I saw nothing but a wall of water on either side of me or the sky. After a few moments, the crest of a wave lifted me.

No boats in sight. To my left, there was a distant coastline.

I was miles offshore! Jeez, how fast did I swim?

The sun was high in the sky, telling me it had been hours since I'd left the house.

I shrugged.

Time worked differently in dreams.

I flipped my tail above the surface like a diving whale to submerge once more. The wind cooled my tail, and I gave a large thrash of it, launching me deeper underwater.

At ninety-nine feet, I reached the ocean floor. A shiver of excitement coursed through me. Never had I so easily reached this depth. In my freediving classes, I had dived to one hundred feet after plenty of preparation.

A bland scene presented itself. Sand covered the ground with the occasional large rock. All the organisms that excited me were closer to shore where the reefs were.

Here, there were fields of sand.

I swam along the bottom, noticing dark brown sea cucumbers. Not that they were actually that color.

When I first got my SCUBA license at twelve years old, I learned the colors of the rainbow dissipated with depth. The light was absorbed, starting with the color red. Needless to say, it made the area rather lackluster.

A motor from a boat buzzed in the distance. Sounds could travel for miles underwater. I had faith it was a decent distance away.

Clanking metal from a crab trap grated through the water every time it hit the benthic bottom.

Putzing along, my mind wandered back to the incident. I rolled my eyes. I couldn't believe for a second I actually thought a mermaid had not only saved me, but changed me into a mermaid too.

Plus, why did my brain insist on torturing me in advance? Honestly, I was down for a cool mermaid dream, but drowning was a crappy thing to put me through.

I chuckled into the water at my stupidity, still managing to surprise myself with how clear it sounded.

I commonly had dreams where I could breathe underwater or swim incredibly fast. But I'd always wake up disappointed at the realization that it wasn't real. Now my mind seemed to be combining the best and worst dreams I'd ever had. This may have been my most realistic dream yet, but a dream nonetheless.

The muscles in my tail flexed a little harder as I quickened my pace, despite having no idea where I was headed.

I'd probably wake up at any moment and feel that same disappointment I always did. But I'd already felt the torture, I might as well enjoy the good part. I had never had a lucid dream before, and I wasn't going to let this be a wasted opportunity.

I veered right toward the shore, or the direction my body seemed to indicate was closer to shore, in hopes of finding an area filled with fish and other marine life.

26

FOUR

Hundreds of fish littered the water, creating a fusion of rainbow specks.

I was now half a mile offshore and under seventy feet of water. I smiled at the life surrounding me. It was surreal.

Herbivorous fish, like damselfish and surgeonfish, ate at the algae-ridden rocks as shrimp hid within the crevices clacking their claws. There were blue and green parrotfish with a stripe of red on their fat upper lip that were courting each other for their midday spawn. A school of silver jacks swam high above, scouting the reef. While brown rockfish sat completely still on the sand in hopes that nothing noticed.

With a trill in my belly, I swam through the community, being brushed now and again by angelfish, which were black with gold flecks and each as large as a dinner plate that could hold a giant slice of pizza.

I dipped and dived; spun and flipped. Enjoying the weightlessness and the graceful movements I had only seen before in dolphins. Movement caught my eye in the distance.

It was probably a fish on the edge of visibility. At least, I sure hoped it was a fish. My stomach twisted with worry that it might be the mermaid.

I shook my head. "It's only a dream," I murmured to myself. Even if she did find me, what's the worst that could happen? I wake up?

The water around me grew warmer where I floated.

Another shadow crossed above me; a lot bigger than before.

When I looked, there was nothing there.

I wrapped my arms around my stomach.

A high-pitched squeal followed by clicking echoed through the water.

My mind began to race. Would the mermaid be mad? What'd the girl want with me anyway? It's just a dream. It's just a dream, I continued to reassure myself.

My eyes were squeezed tight, but flew open when a propulsion of water from something swimming by shoved me to the left.

A pod of dolphins flitted around me.

Laughter bubbled from me. I was way too on edge. The mermaid had spoken English earlier; I doubted she'd revert to whistles and clicks.

"Get a grip," I snorted at myself.

One dolphin swam up to me. He turned his head to the side to stare directly into my eyes. There was a puckered scar across his eye.

Scars on dolphins were common. It could have been caused by an attack from another dolphin or in protection. My eyes traced the rest of the dolphin, where more indents and scars mottled its body. It was clear from the crisscrossing pattern that the imprints were from a net.

Reaching my hand out tentatively, I held the dolphin's gaze. My fingers were a few inches away from one of the deep scars when the entire ocean went silent. I held my breath as I gently placed my hand against its rubbery skin.

The dolphin let out an array of low clicking noises with its mouth open. I could almost believe he was smiling and purring with affection.

I smiled. "Wow," I breathed. "You feel so real."

The dolphin nuzzled my hand.

"All right, dream dolphin, you need a name. What do you think of Poseidon?" I asked.

It squealed in response.

"I'll take that as a 'yes,'" I laughed.

The entire ocean erupted once more, coming back to life. The seven other dolphins of the pod swam in circles around me. They each clacked, reminding me of a playing card thwapping against a bicycle wheel, as they swam to feel the warmth of my hand against them. They were rubbery and gave off no heat, almost like they were more toy than animal.

The dolphins shot up to the surface, jumping into the air, before arcing to come back down with a splash.

Poseidon swam back to me. He nodded his head up and down, pointing his beak at me and then at the sky. He flicked his tail and rose a bit and turned his head back down at me, urging me to join in.

All the other dolphins leapt and dove, breached and bucked.

I swam closer to the bottom, and with a large smile, thrust my tail back and forth. The water became less dense as I neared the surface. With each stroke, I moved faster.

Breaking the surface, I flew into the open air with Poseidon leaping right beside me. I threw my hands out to the side with a light scream before plunging back to the sea.

My entire body soared with exhilaration. Resting my head on the side of Poseidon, I caught my breath. Never in my wildest fantasies had I experienced something like this. Sure, I had seen dolphins from afar, but it felt incredible to play with them, to be a part of their pod. There was this understanding, this camaraderie I'd never thought possible as a human. This was definitely the coolest dream I had ever had.

Poseidon tensed beneath my forehead and released a high-pitched alarm to his pod.

All the dolphins swam directly to him, and after a couple of clicks, they swam off.

Poseidon gave me a nudge in their direction. My fin tensed, holding me where I floated.

"Hey, bud," I said. "I don't want to swim out to the open ocean."

Been there, done that.

Poseidon ticked at me once, and raced after his pod.

Dolphins were finicky creatures. Their sudden alarm wasn't too concerning.

I shrugged, trying not to worry, and sought out my next adventure.

I swam back down to the ocean floor, but the menagerie of fish was gone, hidden. The ocean had become a ghost town. That's when I heard the constant rumbling.

The increasing sound of an approaching engine reverberated through my body.

I tensed, praying they hadn't seen me jump from the water earlier. I rolled my eyes. Seriously? Yes, it felt incredibly real, but did I have to keep reminding myself this was a dream? It didn't matter if they saw me. Unless being caught would wake me. I didn't want that to happen yet. Staying close to the ground would keep me hidden.

I floated along as the vessel grew closer. A distinguishable scraping rumble punctured my ears. It was so tremulous, I could almost feel the metal grating down my spine.

I balled up, and sank to the ground. My hands clutched a large rock beside me while I scanned the surface above.

A few dozen fish of all kinds, shapes, and sizes flew past me in a frenzied stampede.

I looked to my right and saw the fishing boat looming straight toward me.

There was no way they would be able to see me.

Squinting into the water behind the boat, I spotted a gigantic net. The sides were flared out by massive cement blocks on both ends. They dragged along the bottom, leaving destruction in their wake.

The reef, the fishes' homes, were all demolished.

The fishermen were trolling for shrimp, a common practice.

The boat was above me now.

I was frozen, too petrified of being seen.

The net barreled down on me.

I needed to move. Now.

I bolted. The boat was fast, but I was faster. I didn't slow my pace, and I prepared myself to dart to the side to escape from the front of the net.

I passed over a baby sea turtle leisurely swimming in the same direction as me. It wasn't aware of the net creeping toward it.

My heart sank. I couldn't leave the sea turtle. The survival rate of sea turtles was so low already. I had spent years trekking to nests to protect baby sea turtles from seabirds as they raced to the ocean.

I was ready to wake up now. I waited, even going the classic route of pinching myself, but nothing happened. I wasn't waking up. I couldn't float here and do nothing.

I dove toward the sea turtle, but when it saw me sprinting toward it, it dove between some rocks for protection.

I pressed my lips together in annoyance. "I only want to help you," I hissed as I frantically pushed rocks to the side.

The boat got closer, the net barely visible in a sandy cloud with debris flying around it.

The poor sea turtle huddled within the shadows of a crevice.

"Please, come out. I want to help you," I begged.

My heart thumped with every grinding rock and snapping coral behind me.

I backed away from the rocks. A sigh of relief swept through me when the turtle popped its head out.

I turned to flee, but paused. There was no way the turtle could out-swim the net. The turtle wouldn't let me anywhere near it either. If I made a grab for it, it'd dive back into the rocks. The exact ones that would be ripped up any second.

I swam into the cloudy mayhem.

The water was murky from all the particles of the floor. It stung my eyes.

The cement blocks grated across the ground punctuated with loud thunks as they ran into hundred-year-old corals.

My chest tightened at the destruction. I needed to stop it.

The contraption couldn't be that sophisticated. I only needed to unhook the net from the blocks, right? I squinted with blurry vision, irritated by the sand.

But before I could make a move out of the turbid water, I was struck.

The side of the net hit me square in the face.

Face stinging and dizzy, my whole body was forced against the net. The g-force of the pull held me in place.

I dug my fin into the ground, hoping that I could fight the speed of the net. Pain soared through me as bits of rock slashed my fin.

The murky water became a light pink color.

My face contorted as I held back a cry of pain with a clenched jaw. I didn't let up. My hands grasped the bottom of the net in an attempt to not be swooped inside the bell-shaped trap behind me.

This wasn't a dream.

The pain of nearly dying coupled with what I was experiencing now left no doubt in my mind. There was no way this was a dream. I would have woken up by now.

I gritted my teeth as I fought back tears. I hadn't died, but this wasn't a dream. I was a mermaid. And if I was caught...

My chest seized. I couldn't be caught. Who knows what humans would do to a mermaid?

The pace slowed down, lightening the oppressive net against my body.

The engine stopped.

Success!

Flecks of sand flitted about and drifted toward the ground.

I took a few steadying breaths.

The net pulled slightly, raising my fin off the bottom. I toppled, tail overhead, as the cement blocks raised from the ground. I landed in a bed of shrimp and bycatch.

The weight of the wiggling organisms pressed me into the side of the net.

We were caught.

My stomach dropped, and I tried not to hyperventilate. If I didn't die in the process, like most bycatch, and I couldn't change back, I'd be put in an aquarium for the rest of my life or become some science experiment.

Tears welled in my eyes, not fully mixing with the saltwater.

I should be home by now, working on college classes, and getting ready to eat lunch. I wanted to be home with my aunt. She was probably worried sick about me. If something happened to me, she'd never forgive herself. I should've taken out the loan, made her open her restaurant, given her something for everything she's done for me. I'd been cold and distant, it was the least I could have done, and now I might never have the chance. I wish I could apologize, tell her I loved her, tell her thank you for everything.

The ache in my chest was too much to bear. I wouldn't go without a fight.

I flicked the tip of my fin, but the pressure of the animals made it impossible. The weight got worse until I feared my ribs would crack. With the side of my head against the netting, I couldn't even turn my neck.

I couldn't fight it.

Even if I survived being dragged up by the net, I would need to find a way off the boat.

A small boulder slid along the inside of the trap, ramming my head. Spots filled my vision. All I could concentrate on were the fish wiggling against my body as disorientation took hold.

"Here she is! I found her!"

My eyes snapped open. "I'm here," I gurgled.

Four mermaids, or rather mermen, swam up to where I was immobile on the other side of the barrier.

My fingers stretched in their direction through small holes in the net.

They found me! I could be saved.

Through my eyelashes, I looked up and realized I was only fifteen feet from the surface. Time was running out.

"Hold still! I can't help you if you don't hold still!"

I froze, and stared at a merman with shaggy midnight blue hair. His angular jaw cut out from beneath, perfectly matching his broad shoulders. If the god of the sea decided to be a merman, this would be him. His strong dark blue tail swept side to side with determined strokes. He was beautiful but deadly, an apex predator of the ocean.

My insides twisted when his black eyes pierced mine in what seemed like annoyance. This was no teenage boy; he was nothing like the young men I had seen. My mind blanked, losing my ability to speak.

He raised a razored shell to the net. "I need to cut you out."

The opening he created tore easily from the weight of the animals, and I tumbled free.

The merman grabbed my hand, pulling me away.

The net was lifted the rest of the way out of the water with a gaping hole that freed a few more lucky fish. Its tatters landed on the deck with a hard thunk. The sound reverberated into the water and echoed in my pounding head.

My hands shook. That was too close.

I held onto the arm of the merman, cowering from the fate I had almost faced. No one moved, and we all barely breathed, as the boat sputtered forward.

Once out of sight, the merman beside me relaxed with a deep breath that had a hint of a snarl.

I gave a wry smile to the man who had saved me. "Thanks," I murmured.

The corner of his mouth twitched downward in response. "You have no idea the mess you almost caused, not just for yourself, but all of Oceanus." He turned away, "I'm going to kill my sister for this."

I scowled at the back of his head as he swam toward the other three mermen a few tail strokes away who eyed me with pure fascination.

The one on the left had a buzzed haircut that looked like purple fuzz atop his caramel skin. His eyes were a piercing, kelp forest green. He had no shirt of any kind, and his muscles flexed as the tail that matched his eyes flicked side to side. The mass of his tail was as large as his human half. He must have been at least seven feet tall.

The man in the middle gazed warily at me with soft, stormy gray eyes. He was a stockier build, slightly overweight. The type of weight that came from a good home cooked meal, but added to his bulldozer body. His hair, a deep crimson color, was so long that it flowed past his shoulders.

The merman on the right had a lavender tail that gleamed iridescent when the sun hit. His body was lean, muddled with light scars. His Brunswick green hair was pulled back in a tight bun. His eyes matched the color of the tail, but flashed vengeance rather than iridescence.

"What're you looking at?" I folded my arms over my bare stomach and glared, almost embarrassed.

"No need to be rude to the mermen who saved your life." The midnight-blue-haired merman turned back toward me with a stern gaze.

He couldn't have been more than a couple of years older than me, but his commanding demeanor still sent a shiver down my spine.

I rolled my eyes. "You're the one being rude. I thanked you for saving my life, and you snapped at me."

"Maybe we shouldn't have. I'm sure I can hail the boat back," he shot back.

My lips pressed into a hard line.

"Sir, we need to cover our tracks," the purple-haired merman reminded him.

I scoffed. They only saved me to cover their own tails. They should have left me to die alone or be discovered. I would have figured it out on my own, just like I always did. I was a strong, independent woman. I didn't need anyone.

"Don't make me regret saving you." The merman who seemed to be in charge glanced over me. "Follow me."

I didn't budge. "Yeah, I don't think so."

"Look. You can stay here and be stubborn, which'll probably get you killed. Or you can have some hope of survival and come with us."

The 'some' part of that statement didn't calm any of my concern.

"I didn't save you just to kill you. Now, please," he ground out that last word, "come with us. I want to return to the city before it gets too late."

My ears perked at the idea of a city filled with merpeople. My curiosity got the best of me, the tension in my body eased, and I dropped my arms to my side in concession. "Fine."

The merman gave a curt nod before turning away.

Once again, I swam out to the open ocean.

FIVE

We swam for so long that the sun was gone.

I could no longer see the moon streak across the surface of the water at this depth either.

Our pace slowed as the darkness deepened. Only sounds seemed to be alive.

A sudden whoosh of water to my right rammed into me.

Please let it only be the mermen changing positions. What I wouldn't give right now for the comforting sounds of crickets or the hoot of an owl. But no, I get eerie swooshes, clicks, grumbles, and trembles.

I bit my lip in anticipation.

Mermaids. There were mermaids. Like real life freaking mermaids! I was kissed by a mermaid and had become one myself. I don't know if this is the most exciting or terrifying thing to have ever happened to me…or possibly any human.

And they were off my coast, where I had swum for my entire life and I didn't even know it!

How had they managed to stay hidden from humans? There were remotely operated vehicles, sonar, radar and deep submersibles tracking and mapping new areas. This wasn't a tiny planktonic life form. This was a half-human, half-fish that could talk, think, and...and change a human into a mermaid. But considering humans had mapped less than 5 percent of the ocean, it was definitely possible.

I crept closer to the merman in front of me, worried I'd get lost.

The end of his tail swiped across my cheek.

I rubbed away the pain, but said nothing. The change from the monotonous swimming helped keep me awake.

I squinted at the dark figure swimming in front of me. I had no idea where we were headed, and peering into the looming dark waters didn't do much. The swoosh of the merman's tail was the only compass I had.

My tail muscles throbbed. We must have been swimming for a minimum of five hours. At least the pain of the cuts on my tail from trying to stop the boat weren't as bad. Or the ache in the rest of my body simply distracted me from them.

We never stopped. We never spoke. We just swam. I couldn't rely on my sight and my hearing wasn't much help either since it was hard to tell what direction sound came from underwater. It was all so disorienting.

I could tell the mermen changed ranks every twenty minutes. Yes, I counted. It gave me a rough estimate of how much time had passed, but that's all.

A tail knocked my head to the side.

"Watch it!" I grimaced.

"Don't crowd me so much and that won't happen," the timber voice in front of me murmured.

I recognized the voice. It was the young merman who had cut me from the net. The one who could be a Greek god based on both his looks and superiority.

"Maybe I wouldn't crowd you so much if you told me where we were going," I snapped.

"Maybe you should be thankful we're taking you to safety

instead of leaving you here to rot like you humans deserve." The last few words were said so low, I wasn't sure if I'd heard him correctly.

"Then do it." I folded my arms across my chest. I dare them to leave me. I don't need this cocky a-hole helping me.

"You are in the deep ocean, away from anything you know, and there are plenty of dangers. You can't go home as you are even if you could manage to find your way back. You really want us to still leave you?" His tone was haughty, like he was daring me and knew I wouldn't accept.

What I hated most is I wouldn't. My heart sank deeper than the ocean. "No," I whispered.

Mermaids were supposedly fiction, so I had no preconceived notions about them. However, they could be a bit more welcoming. This merman showed such loathing for me, a nuisance not worth his time. I didn't know why he had saved me in the first place.

What if they weren't helping me?

My heart rate picked up.

What if they wanted to get rid of me in a place where my half-fish, half-human body wouldn't be found? A shiver ran down my spine from the bottom of my neck to the end of my tail.

Can't they say something to make this a little bit less terrifying? I'm in the dark with four strange men…well, mermen. If I were on land, I'd be screaming for help in this situation. They could tell me their names, explain where we're going, essentially anything at this point.

Not that I was any better. I wasn't trying to strike up a conversation with any of them either.

I cleared my throat.

The mermen ignored me.

I opened my mouth to speak, but nothing came out. Mild panic set in, triggered by my past trauma. What if I went silent again? It's not like I wanted to stop speaking after my parents' deaths, I just couldn't. There was no other way to explain it. But this time, my will to speak was stronger. So, no. This wasn't the same. I wasn't the same.

"Ma name's Edmound," a gentle voice said beside me. The deep tenor of his voice matched the burly, older redheaded merman.

I jumped in surprise. It was so dark, I hadn't realized he was swimming so close to me.

"I'm Billie," I offered.

"Pleasure to meet ya." There was a hint of a smile in his voice, not that I could see it to confirm.

"So, you all speak…English?" I chewed my bottom lip. I was an idiot. Of course they spoke English; they were doing it right now. But in the hours I had to think about my precarious situation, I was most surprised by how human they all seemed. Shouldn't they speak like whales or something?

"Aye," he said. "As well as plenty of other languages depending where in the ocean we are from."

"There's more of you!" I blurted. "All over the oceans?"

He chuckled. "Of course. The Earth is more water than land after all, an oceanic world."

"True," I murmured. Twice now he had spoken as though it was one massive ocean, instead of divided into many oceans, which is what I had been taught in school.

"Are you surprised?" he asked.

"By which part? The fact that you can communicate with humans or that you're across the world and we have no idea?" I shook my head in exasperation.

"Who said we want to communicate with humans or have you aware of our existence?" The blue-haired man glanced back and scoffed. "We speak human languages as a way to protect ourselves from you."

"Protect yourselves?" I tilted my head to the side. "But we could work together. Imagine the possibilities of helping the ocean if humans and mer—"

"Not possible," the blue-haired guy cut in. "Edmound, please do your duty of escorting our guest. There is no reason to chit-chat with the human."

"Yes, sir." Edmound shifted away from my side, refocused on his task.

I glared daggers into the water in front of me. What a jerk. Who was he to judge me or any human? Especially if they didn't even give us a chance? Hiding away was no way to live your life.

My lips pinched together.

But then, who was I to talk? Isn't that exactly what I had been doing for the last four years?

No one spoke as we continued our journey.

My fingers ached from grinding them into fists. I released a frustrated breath, at myself, at the situation. I wish I had the nerve to swim off. But the merman was right, I had no idea where I was or where I'd go. I'd already managed to nearly get caught and potentially killed and that was during the daylight in waters I knew.

The mermen had already saved me once. If they had wanted me dead, I'm sure they would have ended me by now. I guess I had to trust them to some extent.

But what did I really know about them? They seemed to dislike humans, at least the one in charge did. They spoke English, and existed. That's about all. For all I knew, they could be using me as a peace offering. If mermaids were real, who knew what else was real. There could be a sea god who they wanted to sacrifice me to in order to spare one of their own. Or a kraken! What if krakens were real?

No matter how my mind wandered between acceptance and panic, one thing remained true; I didn't understand why the girl had transformed me in the first place. Why not let me drown?

"Stop!" The godlike merman turned sharply in front of me.

He was inches from my face, but he was still hard to make out in the darkness.

I envisioned his stern face with furrowed brows and pursed lips.

Even with minimal time in the light, I had grown accustomed to his withering stare.

"I can hear the creaks in your bones as you wring your hands. The hitches in your breath—I don't know if they are because you're tired or scared—are also particularly annoying. If we wanted to hurt you, we would have. If you want help then continue to follow us, but I have no problem letting you fend for yourself. None of us feel like cleaning up my sister's mess in the middle of the night, and I'd love nothing more than to be asleep right now."

I held my breath until I was red in the face. What I wouldn't give for a good pillow to scream into. I bit my tongue, fearful that the smallest sound would make them swim off, abandoning me in the pitch-black water.

"Sir, I don't think ye need to shout at the poor girl. She must be scared already," Edmound responded.

The other merman sighed before responding, "Go scout out the next marker or something."

The water encircling me heated a few degrees. My blood boiled. Who did he think he was?

You know what, screw it. I don't care if they leave me because it'd probably be better than being left with this arrogant S.O.B. a moment longer.

"You don't need to talk to him like that. He didn't do anything," I said.

"Excuse me?" The merman in charge reacted.

"I don't know your names. I have no idea where we are going. You keep threatening to leave me behind. And through all of this you expect me to comply and follow you into the oblivion of the ocean. I don't know what kind of mess your sister caused, and what I have to do with any of it, but you aren't giving me anything to work with to make me trust you. On top of that, the one person to show me any kind of decency is being treated poorly. So, I'll say it again because, apparently, you've gone deaf after complaining about the sounds I keep making, do not talk to him like that." My chest heaved.

There was silence. There were no breaths from the others. It was as though the entire ocean was awaiting his reaction.

I folded my arms across my chest, expecting for him to take off or yell back at me.

"My name is Gavin."

I blinked in surprise.

He turned away without another word and continued onward.

At least it was something.

SIX

It had been hours more of monotonous swimming, the mermen silently changing position. Lost in thought, I swam through the dark waters.

A tail swished at my head, and I ducked before getting bashed in the face again. My eyes widened. I could see something! I could see the tail and dodge it!

I looked around, and could clearly distinguish a merman on either side of me, another in front, and a fourth behind.

Gavin was directly to my right, where Edmound had been previously.

I allowed the merman in front of me to swim ahead to put a little distance between my face and his tail.

Without the figure blocking my view, I noticed a blue glow outlining a dark hill.

Light! That's how I could see everyone. But it was nighttime, and the light came from below, not above.

Our pace quickened as we swam up the hill.

Peering over the peak, I gasped.

"Welcome to Oceanus," the leading merman said.

I recognized his voice.

The merman with the long red hair and bulldozer body was Edmound. Faint crow's-feet crinkled from years of smiling. He was older than Gavin. Yet he took Gavin's orders.

Ahead of us was a giant building, or rather palace, two hundred feet tall and glowing with a blue-white light. It was beautiful and ethereal, like every sandcastle a person could ever hope to make, a true piece of art.

The castle walls were made of creamy sandstone, and their milky exterior reflected a blue hue from the shining lights. There were towers shooting out from it. They got thinner toward the top until there was nothing left but murky, bubbling water rising from the tips. Holes were strewn through the massive sandcastle. Some showed a bright blue or were covered by a dark green curtain.

Pearly gates greeted us on our way to the castle. Literally. The front gates to the city were made out of different sized pearls in iridescent shades of blues and greens. My hand reached out and grazed the smooth surface. I remember once learning the way to tell a fake pearl from a real one was to rub it against your teeth. If it felt gritty, it was real. So different from the touch of a finger.

Across the top were winding letters carved from abalone shells: *Uzielaq*.

I sounded out the word on my lips, but was too scared to ask the mermen what it meant.

Sprawling out to the left was a town. I wouldn't consider it a city since I easily saw the end of the town where blank sand melted away into the dark waters. The buildings were made of similar material as the castle, but orange globes emitted light along with the blue. With the dark waters surrounding us, I would expect it to seem ominous, but there was a charm about it that had my head perking up. I wanted to explore it.

My lips pressed into a tight smile. My aunt would have loved to explore it too. I wished she was here with me, seeing this, experiencing this.

Various merpeople swam in the streets, plenty of others swam above the town for a straight shot to their destination. Their light chatter drifted through the water, reaching my ears, but it wasn't uproarious, more like the light chatter of a party.

We continued along a kelp-lined path leading to the front door of the castle.

Awestruck by the castle, I hadn't initially noticed the people tending to the kelp gardens. Other merpeople held spears of fish over their shoulders into the random openings speckling the palace. The holes were different sizes, some could easily fit four merpeople across, while others only allowed an arm to stick through.

They stared as we passed, many giving a small tilt of their head to Gavin.

I wrung my hands when their gazes found me, inspecting the odd mermaid with brown hair. Suddenly, I had swapped places with every fish at an aquarium I had ever been to. Now I was the one inside the glass bowl. At least there weren't any little kids knocking on the glass. I distracted myself by focusing on the castle ahead.

Merpeople swam at various heights, leaving or entering through the random holes scattered about the structure. Doors versus windows didn't seem to be as important here as they were on land. Height and gravity weren't a problem either, so there was no need for a distinction between entries.

My stomach curled when I realized I didn't have the luxury of swimming through a side entrance unnoticed. Instead, I was being escorted right through the main gate. Some of the merpeople paid no attention, but most of them ogled me as I passed. Those who didn't stare outright peered out of the corners of their eyes.

Nerves twisted through my stomach like eels through a coral head. Wooziness took hold. I thought I was going to be sick. I reached under my arm and pinched my skin. The sharp twinge helped me momentarily forget about the nausea.

The merpeople must've known I wasn't a real mermaid. Or

maybe the four burly mermen surrounding me gave it away. I kept my focus on the door ahead, trying to ignore the penetrating gazes.

We neared the front door, made of light brown clay, and it slid inward with a groan.

I kept my head down, staring at the sandy floor, as we entered.

"Edmound, go find my mother. Tell her we found the girl and ask her where we should bring her."

I frowned as Gavin sent Edmound away. But my curiosity got the better of me and I raised my head to look around the great hall we had entered. More holes led to large hallways all the way up to the high ceiling. There were no stairs.

No duh. Everyone can swim.

At the top of the ceiling, a giant glass circle radiated a blue light.

Gavin's brow furrowed in my direction as he leaned against the far wall, arms crossed in front of him.

I turned, staring him straight in the eyes, unflinching.

"Don't get used to being here. My sister's mistake will be righted, and you'll be back on land soon enough," Gavin explained.

"No, she won't! You know we can't just change anyone. There's a reason she was turned into a mermaid," a new voice rang through the waters.

"Yeah, and that reason is you," Gavin grumbled to himself.

I spun around and behind me floated the mermaid who had changed me.

She smiled at me. "Sorry I scared you earlier. I didn't have a chance to officially introduce myself. My name's Veron."

I hesitantly reached out and took the delicate hand she offered me.

"It's short for Veronique, but I hate that name."

The corners of my mouth couldn't help but upturn. "Billie," I said. "Short for Willemina, which I hate too."

She grinned, causing her eyes to become tiny creases.

"Veron, seriously, enough with this belief that people can only be changed if they're meant to be changed. Destiny doesn't exist. We were told this as kids, but we're adults now." Gavin's stern voice echoed loudly.

"Stop being such a prat, Gavin," Veron shot back. Her grimace turned into a grin again when she peered over at me. "Ignore my brother. He can be really rude and takes his merman role a little too seriously."

So, the girl who saved me was Gavin's sister. That's how his sister's mess involved him. My gaze bounced between the two of them. Both their tails and hair reflected shades of blue, but where he was nothing but harsh muscle, she was soft acceptance. Their appearances matched their personalities. I smothered my smile.

"What were you even doing there? It's a long swim, you couldn't have been there by chance," Veron struck her chin out at Gavin before her eyes went wide. "You followed me, didn't you? It might shock you, but I'm not a kid anymore. I can take care of myself."

"We don't have time for this," Gavin spat as the water around him heated. "You have no say in this and you're too immature to understand the consequences. It was a foolish decision. Go back to your room or go hang out with your friends. You shouldn't be here anyway."

"I'm not too immature and it's not like you're that much older! Oh my, a whole two years, what a big deal," Veron mocked as she waved her hands back and forth.

"Stop acting like a child and I'll stop considering you one!" Gavin and Veron were nose to nose, the water around them boiling to match the anger that seeped out of them.

"Well give me chances to do things and—" Veron began.

I grumbled to myself, rolling my eyes. I was tired, confused, my body ached, and I had no idea what was going to happen to me within a matter of minutes. There was no way I was going to spend my time listening to a ridiculous sibling rivalry. They were both acting like children.

There was nothing that could be done about this situation at this exact moment. Bickering wasn't going to help anything except maybe cook some fish for dinner.

The siblings separated a bit with eyes wide in my direction.

Little bubbles formed on my skin, reminding me of water in a pot on the stove before it boils. My eyebrows knotted, and with trembling hands, I rubbed away the tiny bubbles from my skin. They floated upward to the high ceiling until I couldn't see them anymore.

Veron placed a hand on my shoulder, mimicking a deep breath for me to follow, and I did.

The water cooled back to its normal temperature.

"I'm sorry. This must have been a horrible day for you—confusing and, well, it seemed incredibly painful when you turned. By the way, I'm really sorry about that. I've never transformed anyone or even seen it done. I didn't know it would be so violent. We must be making the worst impressions," Veron's violet eyes shined with true guilt.

"Yeah, sorry." Gavin turned his face downward in what was either shame or disregard.

"It's fine," I murmured with a shake of my head. My shoulders slumped. "It's just all a little overwhelming."

Veron grabbed my hand. "If it means anything to you, I'm really happy you're here."

I jolted at the sudden contact and swallowed down my shock at the sudden kindness. I didn't remember the last time someone had held my hand.

I smiled at the mermaid before me. Usually, I hated any kind of consolation, but in this moment, it was exactly what I needed. For the first time in years, a sense of ease prickled at me.

"I'm sure you have tons of questions," Veron continued.

"Actually, I'm surprised you haven't burst out with any questions," Gavin gave me a suspicious look.

I snorted to myself. Like he was the person I would want to ask questions to. It took hours before he even gave me his name, and that was after he threatened to give me back to fishermen or leave me stranded in the open ocean.

His dark eyes bored into me, watching intensely like he was waiting for something.

My eyes traced his sharp jawline, full eyebrows, broad shoulders, and muscled torso. Our gazes locked, and my face heated.

His gaze dropped to my cheeks, then to my lips, for a split second before pulling them away. His mouth downturned with a grimace.

"Wouldn't you have a million questions if you were turned human? She's allowed," Veron interrupted, dropping my hand as she turned to face her brother.

"I would never be human." Disgust filled Gavin's face, his features pinching together.

I glared at him. "Who are you to judge me? To judge an entire species? You don't see me hating all merpeople just because you're a royal ass."

Veron covered her mouth when a giggle slipped out.

Gavin opened his mouth to retort, but Edmound swam down from a hallway above his head, preventing him from saying whatever insulting thing he was about to say.

"Mirah is ready to meet ye in the study," Edmound announced, raising an eyebrow at Veron's sudden appearance. He looked over at me and gave a supportive smile as the color drained from my face.

"Who's Mirah?" I asked.

"Our mom." Veron gave me a thumb's up. "We're on your side, don't worry."

I side-eyed Gavin. Were they? Here was the talk, the decision of what would be done with me, and these were complete strangers.

My life was in their hands, and I didn't know if that was a good thing.

"Seems you'll have to save your questions for my mom." Gavin hesitated before leading the way.

Veron offered a wide, encouraging smile, and we all fell in rank behind Gavin who swam upward toward the blue light.

SEVEN

Mazes of sandy halls bejeweled with pearls, seashells, and blue bioluminescent lanterns made me dizzy with anticipation.

"We're here." Gavin said when we stopped in front of a wooden door.

"It's going to be fine," Veron said as she rubbed my back.

At the friendly touch, my bottom lip trembled.

Veron kept giving me empathetic gestures, reminding me of the comfort of a mother's hug.

I bit my lip to hold myself together, and looked toward Gavin.

His face was stern, but worrying eyes stared at me.

I took a deep breath, unfolded my arms and stuck out my chin. I could do this. I wouldn't go down without a fight. Tiredness no longer seeped through my limbs; instead, they were alive with energy, with a resurgence of determination.

"I'm ready." I nodded.

Gavin's clenched fist landed three loud knocks on the door. Each bang resounded through the hall.

"Come in," a mature female voice answered from the other side.

I followed Veron and Gavin. I had tried to be the last to enter the room, but Edmound remained behind me. It was probably a requirement in case I tried to flee.

Veron and Gavin separated, revealing a wide room littered with antiques. A painting of a woman and her child, not a merperson but an actual human, hung on the wall. There were decaying wooden chairs, rusted anchors, clocks that no longer ticked, a carved mermaid figurehead that took up a quarter of the room, and a rotting wooden desk. It was a collectible room of human objects.

Up against the grainy wall to the left was my snorkel gear. Veron must have grabbed it and brought it back with her after I had swum off.

In the middle of the room, a mermaid sat on a large stone throne. She had long, silvery hair reaching to her lower back. A light green tinge reflected from her silver hairs as though the woman had been in a chlorine-rich pool for too long.

"Mother, this is the human." Gavin finally broke the silence.

I scowled at the introduction. He didn't need to sound so demeaning when he said it, and he could use my name.

"I believe the girl can speak for herself." The mermaid had a rather deep voice for a woman, but there was power in it. She could undoubtedly silence rooms with a single word.

I nodded my head, unsure if that was the cue for me to speak. I stuck out my hand for a handshake. My parents had stressed the importance of good manners from a young age.

The rise of Mirah's thick eyebrows greeted me instead of a hand.

What if she was royalty and didn't shake hands? Was I supposed to bow?

Horrified, I retracted my hand and gave a deep bow.

"That is quite unnecessary." Her sonorous chuckle filled the water. "There is no need for such formalities. We are all…" the woman paused, her eyes taking me in, "…equals here."

I forced a smile, trying to keep my body firm and steady to match the mermaid.

"You seem to have created quite a situation for us."

I frowned. This wasn't my fault. All I had wanted was to get a closer look at a midnight parrotfish. How was I supposed to know I'd get stuck?

I opened my mouth to explain, but stopped. What if the woman didn't know Veron had been the one to turn her? Gavin clearly knew, but they could be hiding it from their mother. Mirah was clearly an authority figure here. Despite everything, Veron had saved my life and I wasn't going to be the one to condemn the mermaid supportively floating at my side.

"Calm down," the woman breathed toward me.

Crap, I guess I wasn't as calm and collected as I thought.

"I don't need an explanation from you, although I'd like one from my daughter." Her eyes, the color of gray storm clouds, shifted over to Veron. "You know it is forbidden to go so close to shore, and then you do this? Explain...it." A long slender hand waved in my direction.

"I am so incredibly sorry, Mother," Veron began. "I know I'm not supposed to go near shore, but I was looking for a gift for Dad's birthday. I hadn't realized how close I was to the shore. And then I was intrigued when I saw the girl dive down to pick up the junk on the ocean floor. I'm used to people dumping things instead of picking them up. The next thing I knew, she was drowning! I panicked. All I could think about were the stories about changing someone. You used to tell me that only one whose destiny truly lies within the ocean can change. I knew I was her only hope." Veron's face flushed pink as she inhaled deeply.

"You didn't think to just untie her?" Gavin said under his breath so only Veron and I could hear.

"If it could have just been untied, I would have done it myself," I mumbled as I glowered at him. My hand flew to my mouth, realizing I had spoken a little too loudly. Sound traveled so much more easily underwater.

Mirah stared down at me, and I backed up. Gavin hadn't said it loud enough for his mother to hear, but here I was interrupting for all to hear. Instant regret filled me. The need to protect Veron flared in my chest. She had saved my life.

"Miss…" I hesitated. My hands shook at my sides.

The mermaid on the throne inclined her head. There was no turning back now.

"Please do not be angry at Veron for this," I continued.

"And why do you say this?" Mirah stared down her nose as her fingers drummed on the armrest. Her eyes didn't leave my face, didn't even blink, inspecting me while waiting for my answer.

My body rippled with adrenaline. A knot formed in my stomach, instinct overpowering my logic. I counted back from five, clearing my mind and relaxing the muscles in my body. It was something my aunt taught me before sending me to therapy. My chest pulled with the reminder of her, but I pushed away my longing for her, for something familiar. If I ever wanted to see her again, I needed to survive.

"Well?" Mirah's impatient voice rang out.

With a final puff, I said, "I am incredibly grateful that she saved my life. You should be proud that you have a daughter who cares so deeply about the life of someone she doesn't even know. But if there's a way to turn me back, do it! I don't want to cause problems, and I swear that I will not speak a word of this to anyone. Ever." I stared into Mirah's stoic face, and pushed every ounce of sincerity into my eyes.

"Yes, that would be an easy way to solve the situation except there is no known way to 'unchange' a transformed human." She sat quietly in her seat, contemplating with a furrowed brow and a finger twisting through her hair.

I peeked over at Veron who mouthed "Thank you." I had quickly taken a liking to Veron; she was exceedingly sweet, so unlike her brother. Glancing toward Gavin, his intense stare caught mine, causing another shiver to roll down my spine to the tip of my tail.

I was ready to face the consequences. Whatever the decision was, I wouldn't fight it as long as nothing happened to Veron. "Miss Merqueen?" I said.

"Merqueen?" Again, this daunting woman smirked. "You may call me Mirah. I may have a more authoritative role here in Oceanus, but I am nowhere close to a queen. Nor do I wish to be. And now that we are exchanging formalities, may I request your name?" Mirah lifted herself off of the chair and swam over to me. She was incredibly tall. The size of the throne had concealed her true height, but she was easily a foot taller than my meager five foot five inch stature. Although, I wonder if I had acquired a couple more inches after gaining a tail.

"My name is Billie." I clenched my jaw and held my chin high.

"That's an…interesting name," Mirah loomed.

I stammered, no longer feeling the power of her voice. "It's short for Willemina, Willemina Farraige." I scanned Mirah's face and watched as she took in some water through her mouth. Was she thinking, gasping, or drinking? I couldn't tell, and I was too nervous to ask, even if I was super curious about how mermaid anatomy worked.

"Okay. For now, it seems she will be staying with us. I will spread the word and we will pull together a communion with the council to be held tomorrow. This is not a decision that is only up to me. Having her here could have consequences that affect everyone. Thus, everyone should have a say. Veron and Gavin, find her a room to sleep in."

My shoulders squeezed together. My fate would lie in the hands of people who stared at me like I was a total freak. This was hopeless. There was no way I was going to survive this.

"We're going to have so much fun!" Veron chimed in as though I wasn't doomed. "I know you must be exhausted, so let's find you that room." Veron grabbed my hand and dragged me toward the door.

"Make sure you find her some appropriate clothes. A new face is trouble enough," Gavin added.

I still wore my green bathing suit top, the most human thing about me. Well, that and my brown hair.

Veron, on the other hand, wore a blue sea star patterned tube top woven of plastics.

"I'd actually prefer to stay in my bathing suit top," I admitted. By this point, it was the only thing keeping me linked to home.

"There are enough problems arising from this. It'd be much easier if you fit in a little more," Gavin grumbled.

"Well, what if I don't want to fit in?"

"I don't think you need to," Veron voiced admiringly.

"Let the girl keep her clothes," Mirah said. "In due time, son, things will work out. She will be noticed whether she wears our clothes or not."

Once again, Veron was dragging me from the study and off to find me a room for my stay in Oceanus.

EIGHT

"**H**ey, you awake?"

I pried open my eyes to see Veron peeking around the door into my new room.

The room was fairly simple. I was lying on a purple sponge mattress that conformed to the curves of my body. There was a stone chair in the corner underneath a large window covered by kelp that grew up from the bottom of the sill.

How it grew without sunlight was a mystery to me. I could only assume it was a type of deep-sea kelp which had yet to be discovered by humans. My parents had always dreamed of discovering a new species and naming it themselves.

There were strings on either side of the window to tie the kelp curtain back. On the far wall across from my bed was a hole where the murky, bubbling water rose. It must have been the same water I had seen shooting out of the tips of the towers the day before.

"Barely," I grumbled, rolling back over and closing my eyes.

"You haven't eaten in over twenty-four hours. I imagine if you put food in your stomach it'd help." Veron plopped down in bed next to me.

"What time is it?" I mumbled.

"It's almost half day."

Half day. Without working watches, it made sense they didn't keep time in the same manner.

Veron handed over a plate of food. "There's some cooked seaweed and snapper. I wasn't sure how you felt about eating raw food, so I cooked it for you in a hydrothermal vent."

I peered at the black-green clump with a tinted white fish sitting on top, "This looks great. For the record, I love sustainable sushi, so raw fish doesn't bother me."

I took a bite of the fish. A fresh aroma erupted as it melted in my mouth. The seaweed was a bit on the salty side, but had a pasta-like quality to it. My grumbling stomach died down. The food was magnificent.

"My aunt would love this," I said between mouthfuls.

Veron raised an eyebrow at me.

My hand paused above the food, which shifted easily on the plate with less gravity. "She, uh, is a really wonderful cook." My stomach twisted, staving off my hunger.

I would not cry. I would not cry. But…I missed her, and I hated that she didn't know if I was okay.

"Do you think there's a way to send her a message?" I asked. "You know, to let her know I'm okay."

Veron didn't answer right away, and hope blossomed inside my chest, but when I looked up, her facial features hung in an apologetic frown.

"I'm sorry." She shook her head. "We can't. It's too risky."

"I understand." Truly, I did, but it didn't make it hurt any less. She was all alone. I had left her all alone the way my parents had left me, except I wasn't actually dead. It was unfair to her. Putting the plate down on the bed, I swam to the window, pushing the seaweed aside. The view was spectacular. I hadn't realized how high I was.

In the distance, I could see the tip of the ridge we swam over to enter Oceanus. Merpeople worked busily in the anemone gardens and children played tag with eruptive giggles. The only way I could tell it was no longer night was that, instead of black waters, the waters had become a deep blue.

We must be at least one thousand feet underwater! That made sense since mermaids had been able to live incognito from the human world.

Veron's watchful gaze prickled the back of my neck. My fingers knotted together, but Veron said nothing. The tension built until I couldn't handle it any longer.

"What is it? Just tell me," I exhaled.

Veron shifted uneasily. "Everyone is meeting today. To decide what to do with you. I know my mom said it'd be today, but I hoped it'd take longer to get everyone together. Word spread incredibly fast. Oceanus wanted to gather to make the decision as fast as possible."

Yeah, as fast as possible to get rid of me. I rubbed my hands on my lap, feeling the polished scales beneath.

"I'm sure it'll be fine. Merpeople just like to be really productive is all. They probably just want to get it over with so they can continue on with their day. It'll be no problem," Veron forced reassurance.

"Yeah, I'm sure it won't," I feigned.

"Gavin will be there too," Veron added. "He's a future council member, so he requested to attend."

"Great." Sarcasm coated my voice.

"He'll have your back." Veron nodded.

I pursed my lips. Gavin would have Veron's back, but I doubted he would have mine.

"I wasn't sure if you would want to make yourself a little more presentable. I brought you these just in case." Veron passed me a pile of objects.

An ordinary comb I assumed someone had scavenged from the litter humans put in the ocean, an orange and pink spiral shell with a string through it, a barnacle, and a chunk of live purple sponge.

"I know what the comb is for, but what am I supposed to do

with these?" I held up the stringed shell, purple sponge, and black barnacle.

"The shell is a headband for your hair. It'll look nice on you and it's a popular hairdo for a lot of mermaids. The barnacle is to brush your teeth, and the sponge is to scrub your body. It feels great against your scales."

"Thanks." I removed my hairband and let my brown knotted mess of hair float around. Running the comb through its lengths, I detangled it to the best of my ability, but as soon as one knot disappeared, another formed.

I froze when I noticed it had a slight blue-green tint to it. When did that happen? My hair didn't have deep colors like Veron's or Gavin's hair, but it wasn't its usual shade of brown. Either way, I'd still be instantly singled out as an outsider.

I snagged the barnacle and thought of all the encrusted barnacles usually found attached to the stilts on piers. Sticking something like that in my mouth seemed disgusting. I couldn't bring myself to do it. I placed it back on the bed between me and Veron.

"Do you want me to help you with the shell?" Veron asked.

"Yes, please."

Veron picked up the strings from my lap, and I turned to face the other way. I stared at the blank wall, trying to clear my mind.

"Voila!" Veron thrust a broken piece of mirror in front of my face.

I grabbed it out of her hands, careful not to cut myself on the edges. My odd-colored hair floated out to the sides, and when I moved my head to one side, my hair slowly shifted around me. The orange and pink shell sat above my temple, holding back my hair so it wouldn't float into my face.

Veron smiled over my shoulder in the mirror.

"Thank you. It's beautiful." I gave her a sheepish smile.

"Are you sure you don't want to eat any more before we go?" Veron frowned at the plate with about three-quarters of the food still left.

"Wait, we're going now?" I tensed.

"I figured we should get there early. You could prepare. Although, I'm sure it'll be fine."

"Yeah, okay." I nodded. I knew what she meant. I needed the time to mentally prepare for what could happen; my life was still in their hands.

Swimming through the halls, I felt like an ant swarming through an anthill filled with monotonous passageways. I had no sense of direction. Veron must have a sixth sense with how she navigated this maze. My mind was a frazzled mess by the time Veron came to a halt in front of a fifteen-foot-tall door made of wooden planks.

Veron squared her shoulders and pushed the wooden door open, her tail swishing in broad strokes. Time to walk the plank.

We entered a gigantic indoor arena. Encircling three-quarters of the room were rows of sand, piled and pressed into stadium seating. Small blue lights littered the walls, creating a dim light throughout the chamber. In the center, a circle of lava globes lit the flat ground and one large bioluminescent light hung right above the area with a rock placed at its center.

It reminded me of the time my parents took me to see an off-Broadway production of *The Lion King*.

My insides twisted as if they were filled with a gaggle of lampreys—slimy, eel-like fish that had funnel-like sucking mouths in order to feed on their prey.

"I'd suggest floating over there until they call you forward," Veron pointed to a dark area where the aisles were separated by a closed door. "The door goes to an empty side room. No one should be going in or out. Would you like me to stay with you?"

I shook my head. Despite having a constant supply of water, my throat felt dry.

Veron looked at me the way all of my friends had looked at me when they heard about my parents.

The same glimmer of pity, the silence of awkwardness, and the pout of pain. Veron turned and left the room.

A part of me hated her for a split second. I was in this position because she turned me, and she still took the time to pity me.

I pressed myself up against the coarse, sandy wall.

Merpeople entered the arena. At first there were only a few, but as time went on, hordes of them filled the stands. Merpeople with fins of various blues, browns, and burgundies. They had wild hair—twisted, vibrant, and alive. The waters coursed with energy.

The merpeople yammered, and as I looked through the stands, I realized I was the youngest person here. I yearned for anything familiar, anything that would give me confidence or hope. In the middle of the front row, eyes so dark they seemed to have no pupils gazed at me.

Gavin.

I met his stare.

He sank down to his seat. The tips of his firm mouth raised into a light, supportive smile. It seemed like an odd gesture coming from him and looked unnatural on his face.

I couldn't force a smile of my own. I was so nervous I thought I might hurl.

Gavin took a large breath and slowly blew out through his mouth, his hands emphasizing the gesture.

I mimicked his actions and the muscles in my tail became less twitchy. Taking deep breaths of the water, I was surprised how it relaxed me in ways that air never did. I tore my eyes away from him and looked down at my mysterious tail.

The end had been continuously twitching back and forth, and I hadn't even realized it. I took another deep breath and watched as the involuntary movements died down until the only thing shifting the soft fibers was the water current.

I glanced back up. Gavin no longer watched me, but a small smile graced his lips.

I needed to stay calm. If I showed fear, I would seem guilty. I had done nothing wrong. They needed to believe that I didn't mean them any harm, and I didn't. But it was obvious they didn't trust humans, and their need to protect themselves might outweigh my own safety.

I straightened my back.

Worst case scenario, I'd bolt; that was my plan. The ocean was huge, and as long as I could find my way out of this sandcastle, I would find a way to hide. There were options, and I would do whatever I needed to survive.

"Will you please come to the center with me?" A large merman, easily seven to eight feet tall with the inclusion of his dark blue tail was speaking. His hair was a faded white-blue. His face was composed almost to the point of boredom. There was no light in his eyes or energy in his voice.

"Isn't there an introduction to what's happening or something?" I pressed for more time.

"We all know why we're here, and everyone would just like to get on with it," he replied straight-faced.

Veron was right; the merpeople really did like to be proactive.

I swam upward until I was eye-level with him, ready to stick up for myself, but I paused.

The only reason for exiling me would be because I seemed to be a threat. A threat to their community and way of life, an inconvenience. I needed to seem meek and uninteresting, someone who wasn't going to pose a problem.

I sank back down to the ground, hunched my shoulders, and faced the ground. I would make myself seem unimportant, a simpleton, someone who wasn't even worth the merpeople's time.

He started toward the middle of the arena.

Keeping my head bowed and hands interlaced in front, I followed him.

The merman gestured for me to take a seat on the rock in the middle of the stage area.

My stomach dropped.

NINE

The rock was uncomfortable, bumpy in all the wrong places. It tipped toward the right, so I had to continuously move my tail to keep my balance.

I needed to sit up straight, shoulders back. What should I do with my hands? I tried to use them to help me balance on the rock, but there wasn't any purchase for them, so I curled them together in my lap. I was a real fish out of water. The thought nearly made me laugh. Perfect, just what I need, ill-timed jokes to make me laugh like a lunatic.

I stole a glance toward the audience around me, but saw only darkness. The lights surrounding me made it impossible to see what was beyond them. I was a performer on stage, to be ogled and ridiculed. The problem was…I had stage fright.

The merman stayed in the circle, floating nearby without speaking another word. Paralyzing silence made it impossible to know how many people were staring at me.

"We all know," the merman stammered. He coughed, clearing his throat, and began again. But his voice had no strength the way Mirah's had. Instead, he rushed to get it over with. "We all know why we are here. I will not bore everyone again with the details of how this came to be, the fact of the matter is that it did. We are gathered now because a single merperson may not decide what to do with this girl. Having her here is a choice that could impact everyone in Oceanus. It is time to discuss these matters, take everything into consideration, and make a decision." The second he ended his speech, the darkness erupted in voices.

"What shall we do with her?"

"We should get rid of her!"

"She's only a girl."

"Why was she saved in the first place?"

"She must have been turned for a reason!"

My attention darted into the darkness wildly. There was no distinguishing who was talking, and most of the noise was murmuring in the background. Some voices continued to shout above the general crowd.

It took every ounce of courage I had not to speak up. I might not like the attention, but sitting by and letting my fate be decided by a group of strangers was even worse. Still, I couldn't risk saying the wrong thing or making myself seem like a threat. I squeezed my hands together so tightly, my knuckles turned white. All I wanted to do was disappear at that moment. All this attention on me made me feel sick.

"Who turned her?"

"Use her for chum."

"Send her back to the humans!"

"She could help us with our problems!"

"She *is* one of our problems!"

"Enough!" A voice in the audience to the right echoed louder than the rest—Gavin. Thankfully, the hall quieted after this loud, decisive intrusion. "If this girl had not been saved, she would have died. I am the one who saved her from the net. Why? Because if she had been found out, we all would have been found out! Everyone knows that humans don't just turn into one of us. For a long time, even the possibility was thought to be a myth. However, within this myth is the belief that if a human was turned, there was a purpose for their transformation. A reason. That reason may not be clear now. It is like the thousand-mile journey sea turtles make in order to lay their eggs where they were once birthed. It is not known why they pass plenty of perfectly good birthing grounds, but they always return to their place of origin. Maybe that is what is happening here. Maybe the ocean is telling us that this girl needs to be here. Even if it is not understood now, that is no reason to condemn her."

Surprise at his declaration slammed into me, stealing my breath. No, he was protecting Veron, not me.

"But she's a human! She can't be trusted!" a random voice rang out.

"Aye, that is true," Gavin responded. "However we have spent most of our lives hiding from humans, misunderstanding them as they do us. As they do the ocean. Perhaps, this is a chance instead of a threat. Not to say it won't be challenging, but it could be a true gift if we respond rightly."

The arena was silent for minutes before low whispers began. The whispers slowly turned into debates, but luckily no one was shouting this time.

The merman who had introduced me shrunk out of the limelight.

I was alone. Again.

My throat tightened. I wouldn't cry. Not here. Not in front of all these people.

The voices lessened until only a handful continued speaking in hushed whispers.

This was it. This was the final discussion that would decide my fate.

"Billie," a familiar voice floated through the water in a whisper.

I perked up at it, unsure how Gavin was talking to me without everyone hearing.

"Remember to breathe," he added.

I searched the darkness for him, following his advice.

"A decision has been made." The merman reentered the lighted ring. "After our discussion, it has been decided that this human will be done with…"

My chest clenched, and I momentarily forgot to breathe. My heart hammered in my chest. I was done; they were actually going to kill me. Panic set in.

"…her human self. She will be accepted into this mer community as one of our own. She will learn our ways and help protect us the way we've always protected each other. It won't be easy, and it will take work. However, we have decided to give her the chance to become a true mermaid," the merman finished. "In return, she will help us understand humans and answer some of our pressing concerns about her species."

I blinked in complete disbelief. They were going to let me live? Not only that, but they were going to let me live as one of them? I was safe?

I blew out a breath into the water, and small bubbles popped out.

But this meant I was done with my human life. Everything I had ever known was gone. I'd never see my aunt or graduate from college. I would never get to travel with her or eat her delicious pasta. I'd never dance around the kitchen listening to Michael Jackson as I did the dishes, while she rolled her eyes at me before bickering over what movie to watch. She would never see me grow up, have kids…she wouldn't even know I was alive.

My bottom lip quivered, but I bit down on it, refusing to show any emotion. I would live. And I would live in the place I loved the most, the ocean.

Merpeople left the large room, yammering and hurrying back to their duties, while I sat on the rock in silence.

"Congratulations," Gavin entered the blue ring of light. "If it means anything, I'm glad that they didn't feed you to the sharks."

My eyes widened in horror. "Huh?" I uttered.

He chuckled, and my shoulders lifted at the sound like all the weight of the world had been taken off them with a single sound. He had never laughed before, always too serious and cranky, but now I couldn't fathom why he didn't do it more. Maybe he wasn't as dower as I thought.

His eyes crinkled on the sides from his smile. "I'm only messing with you. Sharks don't like the taste of merpeople. It's the giant squid you have to look out for. Come on, let's go find Veron. I know she'll be thrilled with the news."

"Umm…" I wrung my hands as he raised an eyebrow at me. "Thanks for sticking up for me."

His face softened, eyes darting toward the merman who had introduced me earlier. Something flashed across his face, hardening it once more. "Don't get me wrong, I think what my sister did was idiotic, but I needed to protect her. Also, you were never given a choice and you shouldn't be condemned for something you had no control over. Plus, we can utilize your knowledge of humans." His wavy blue hair floated to momentarily cover his eyes.

"Right," I breathed.

"Let's go. I'm sure Veron's waiting just outside," he said.

I followed him back toward the door I'd entered through, but the large merman blocked their path.

"Gavin, even though the girl is safe for now, there is still a lot she needs to learn to fully be accepted or understood. I'm leaving it up to you and your sister to make sure she integrates well. There's no telling what will happen if she doesn't succeed."

"Yes, Father," Gavin nodded, keeping his eyes on the ground.

My eyes widened as my head snapped between the two of them. Trying to break the tension slowly rising in awkward silence, I thrust my hand out to the older merman. "Hi, um, I'm Billie."

Gavin put a hand on my outstretched arm and lowered it. "This is my father, Raiden."

I blushed, remembering his mother didn't return my handshake either.

The older merman frowned down at me with a blank stare.

I bit my lip. I would need to ask Veron about the formalities of meeting someone for the first time.

"I knew it! I knew you'd be okay!" Veron leapt onto me and threw her arms around me.

Speak of the devil.

Raiden used the distraction to leave the three of us alone.

"Yeah, you were right. Sorry I ever doubted you." I gently hugged her back.

"You doubted me?" Veron pulled away with a pout.

"Well, I mean...I didn't necessarily mean doubt...I just," I fumbled.

"It's okay. I'm surprised you didn't cry. If it were me, I would have been sobbing the entire time," Veron cut in.

"That makes me feel a whole lot better." I rolled my eyes. Hearing that a mermaid born and raised here would have been terrified wasn't comforting. I'm definitely happy she told me this after it was over.

Veron let out a little giggle and dragged me by the arm like always. "You want an official tour? Oh! I can show you some of the latest fashions. Or do you want to..." Veron happily bounced along.

"Actually, if you don't mind, I'd really just like to sleep."

"But you slept for so long already," Veron whined, turning to face me with a pleading look.

"Let her be, Veron. You now have all the time in the world to drag her around the ocean." Gavin pulled his sister's hand off my arm.

"Fine." Veron looked sullenly at the ground.

Two against one.

"We can do something tomorrow. Whatever you want," I

chimed in with an encouraging smile.

Immediately, Veron's face was covered by her giant smile before she nodded and swam off.

"Have a nice night," Gavin said.

"Wait!" I scratched my arm and gave an awkward laugh. "Umm. I don't know where my room is."

Amusement sparkled in his dark eyes. "Follow me and pay attention this time. I can't be showing you to your room every time." He cocked his head to the right in the direction of one of the ten passageways.

Yeah, I'd definitely have gotten lost.

"How do the small blue lights work?" I asked as we swam. "I don't expect you have electricity here, but there's light."

Gavin's intense gaze bored into me. "The lights occur due to bioluminescence. Although, we do have a form of electricity too."

I learned about bioluminescence in my marine biology class. It's when a living organism produces and emits light via a chemical reaction. On land, it happens with fireflies, but they light up a yellow-green color instead of this heavenly pearlescent blue.

"Wow, that's amazing." I smiled at the lights we passed, at the tiny organisms I couldn't see but knew were there. "What's the electricity part?"

"Eels," he responded.

"Eels?" My head snapped over to him.

He was staring up at the ceiling, just like I was. "Yeah, electric eels. You know *those* exist, right?" Gavin smirked at me.

"Ha-ha-ha. Very funny." I glared, but if I were on land that smile would have me tripping over myself. It was nice for it to feel easy to be around him for once. "Yes, I know electric eels. They're not half-land animal and half-water animal. They're a bit more believable."

"Whoever said we're half-land animal? Maybe you're actually the mythic creature and we're normal," he retorted.

I rolled my eyes, ignoring his comment, but couldn't stop the pull at the corner of my lips. Did I dare say he was kind of funny? "So, what're these real electric eels used for?" I asked.

Gavin let out a short, triumphant laugh. "For whenever we need an electric current."

He shook his head with a smile before moving on.

I switched between staring at the sconces along the wall and the merboy who slipped through the water with ease. Was it weird I found him handsome? With his sharp jaw and full lips, it would be hard for anyone to not have their breath stolen when looking at him. And for once, he wasn't rigid with tension. His shoulders were relaxed, and arms hung at his side. This was a side of Gavin I wanted to get to know.

The hall became a little more familiar, and we were at my door within seconds.

"Thanks for standing up for me earlier," I murmured as we paused outside my room.

"It was nothing. I'm just looking out for my sister. And just to be clear, even though my dad said I had to take care of you, I have enough responsibilities, so please, don't be too needy."

This merman was going to give me whiplash with his mood swings. My brow furrowed. Needy? I wasn't needy, and he didn't know me well enough to make assumptions.

"Oh, I'm so sorry to be such an inconvenience to your busy schedule. I don't need your help. Not then, and not now. All I was saying was thank you for helping me, not that I needed it." My words were laced with annoyance.

"That's not what I was trying to get at. I have things to do and wanted to make sure you know you can go to others besides me and my sister. You need to learn to integrate yourself into the community, which means relying on more than just a couple of us," he responded less harshly.

"Well, I don't need to rely on anyone or anything."

"You'll learn, Billie. Everyone relies on others, even humans."

Gavin stared at me intently, making me shift side to side in the water.

"I'm not a human anymore. That was made clear. That life is over." A wave of frustration pulled at me, tautening my muscles. This was all so much. I didn't want attention or to be reprimanded or given advice. I had learned to take care of myself, to be independent. I had grown used to not having friends and not relying on others. I should've known better. Clearly, I was meant to be alone in this world. First my parents, then my aunt…why even try?

"No, you're not human anymore. So, you need to learn." Gavin folded his arms over his chest, back to his usual rigid stance.

"Never mind, you don't get it." I deflated. This was exhausting. All of this was so exhausting. "Have a good night."

Gavin shook his head, clearly disappointed in me.

Trust me, buddy, no one could be more disappointed than me right now.

"Rest well," he said and swam away.

My chest heaved as I shut the door behind me, thankful for the peace and quiet, the lack of judgmental stares. I leaned against the wall and burst into tears.

TEN

"Where are you taking me?" I asked for the fifth time. I was given one day of solace, one day to rest and process everything that had happened. On the second morning, this morning, I was rudely awakened by Gavin and told to follow him.

Gavin paused and finally acknowledged my question. "You may have gotten through the trial and been allowed to live, but it doesn't mean the mer council doesn't still have questions. You are a way for us to understand the human world directly from the source itself."

I folded my arms over my chest. "Or you could initiate a conversation with the human race in general, instead of relying on me."

His face soured more, which I didn't think was possible. "That isn't a good idea. We don't have any reason to believe humans would take our existence well or in a humane way," he said. "I suggest you cooperate to make this easier on everyone."

"Or what?" I narrowed my eyes.

He was right. I, also, didn't believe humans would initially react well to an entire cognizant species right under their noses. But humans also weren't monsters, and it bothered me that I kept being painted as one.

He sighed, running his hand through his blue hair. "Or nothing. But you were allowed to live. In good faith, you should try to help the mer community, and not make them regret their decision."

I chewed my bottom lip. He was right again, which was annoying. If I had any hope of surviving this and learning to be a part of the community, then I needed to make an effort.

"Fine," I said.

He nodded, and continued on his way as I followed closely behind.

The halls were as confusing as ever, and I couldn't place where we were in the castle even if my life depended on it.

The bioluminescent orbs lessened until there were more shadows than light.

Eerie.

We ended up in front of a metal door at the end of a hallway.

Gavin motioned for me to enter.

I hesitated.

"Try to cooperate," he murmured.

"Easy for you to say," I whispered back. With a deep breath, I swam forward, and Gavin opened the door for me.

The inside of the room was blank. Completely empty. No windows, chairs, tables—nothing. Compact sand with more sand. The water felt stagnant, and I choked on it upon entering.

"What are we—" I cut off when Gavin knocked twice on the door, and a lock slid into place on the other side. "What the hell was that?"

My lungs tightened as claustrophobia set in. I had never experienced it before, but being locked in this cell had my breaths coming short.

Gavin interlocked his hands behind his back and paced the room. "Have you ever heard of mermaids before?"

I blinked in confusion. "Huh?"

"Answer the question."

"Gavin, what is this?" My nails dug into my palms as I tried to quell my rising panic. "Let me out of here."

When he turned to me, his face was void of emotion. "We cannot leave until you answer the questions."

My mouth opened and closed like a fish out of water. "Please, let me out." My head swam.

"I can't do that," he said. "Answer the question."

"I…I…in stories," I stammered. "In stories, I knew of mermaids. You were nothing but fiction."

He nodded once and continued pacing, not meeting my eyes. "What about others? Aside from fiction, are there humans who believe we are real?"

"There's videos and—"

Gavin paused, shoulders tensing.

I gulped. "But they're conspiracies," I squeaked. "Mockumentaries and photos which are hard to make out. Nothing the general population believes," I squeaked.

He waited.

"I swear!" My eyes widen with alarm. "Even knowing you're real now, I would still think the footage was a lie. Mermaids are myths for us."

Gavin pressed his flat palm against the metal of the door, and closed his eyes. "Do humans know how they are impacting our ocean?"

A breath whooshed out of me, glad to be done with that question. "Yes!" I hold my head higher. This was my chance to help them see that humans weren't terrible. "We have entire organizations dedicated to ocean conservation. They raise money to clean up polluted areas, enact laws to protect endangered species, and try to spread awareness about global warming. Some scientists have even made machines to help with plastic pollution."

Gavin lifted his head, and when he looked at me his face displayed nothing but anger. "You have entire organizations dedicated to helping the ocean. But why do those organizations even need to exist? How do you think species became endangered in the first place? Why do you think global warming is happening? Why do they need to lead clean ups and create technology to reduce trash? Why do you think entire fish species are being wiped out? Our food source!"

I had nothing to say. My stomach flipped as I searched for an answer.

"Humans. You are simply trying to clean up a mess you created, and not very well at that," he added.

"W-we didn't know," I mumbled.

"You didn't? What about now?" His voice echoed through the empty room. "You have the knowledge now, yes?"

"I—"

Gavin interrupted. "It's a yes or no question. Do you possess the knowledge now to know how humans impact the ocean?"

"Yes." The word was like acid on my tongue. It hurt to admit it, but I couldn't lie about this.

"How is plastic made?"

I startled. "What?"

"You just said you possess knowledge on how you impact the ocean. Tell us how plastic is made."

"I meant the human race," I corrected. "I only have a high school degree. I don't know how plastic is made."

"Is plastic harmful to humans too? Or only to the creatures in the ocean?"

"It doesn't wrap around our necks if that's what you're asking," I answered.

Gavin's gaze poured over me, waiting. My response wasn't what he was looking for.

I pressed my fingers to my forehead and sighed. "I understand why you are upset. I do. Humans can really suck sometimes, but we aren't all bad. There are so many of us who are trying. We recycle. We are finding alternatives or veering away from single use plastics. We aren't perfect, but no one is. We are trying our best."

"Are you?" His voice is quiet, filled with a pain I didn't fully understand. "I'll ask again, is plastic harmful to humans too?"

I threw my hands in the air. "I don't know what you want from me! Maybe if you weren't performing some creepy interrogation and were open with me then I could help you!"

"We want you to answer the question!" he hollered back.

My mind blanked. "We?"

The snick of the lock filled the silence.

Gavin moved aside as the door swung open.

"I think that's enough." Mirah waltzed in, head held high.

What the hell?

She stared down her nose at me. "I'm sorry for the unpleasant experience, but the tactics were insisted upon by the council."

I narrowed my eyes at Gavin. I had thought he was on my side, or at least, I had thought that previously. Yet, here he was doing the council's bidding and treating me like a traitor.

"I didn't ask for this," I said. "I didn't ask to be changed. I didn't ask to be saved."

"Yet you were," Mirah said. "You are a mermaid now with unique knowledge of the human realm. Answer me this, do you identify as a mermaid? Do you feel you are one of us?"

I scratched my arm as my brain grasped for the answer she wanted to hear. But she'd know I was lying. "No," I admitted.

"That is exactly why we had to do this." Another voice joined the conversation. A large merman, his height encompassing all of us, filled the doorway. A sharp face with narrowed eyes glared down at me. His midnight black hair was tied up into a bun, arms folded over his muscular chest. He looked to be in his forties and able to take down a grizzly bear.

"Councilman Jerod." Gavin bowed his head at the merman.

The merman ignored him; his attention riveted on me. "Humans are deplorable, an infection spreading across the globe, ruining everything in their wake."

Mirah frowned, but didn't object.

"I'm sorry for what humans have done…are doing," I amended. "But I am one girl. I do not speak for the entire human race, and I do not agree with many of their actions. And I have answered your questions to the best of my ability."

Mirah and Jerod looked at one another, something silent passing between them.

"Very well," Mirah conceded. She looked toward Gavin. "She is free to go. You may take her back to her room."

I swam forward, shoving past Gavin. "Don't bother. I'll find my own way."

He was the last person I wanted to be around.

ELEVEN

I had just about given up on finding my room when a friendly face came into view.

"Veron!" I called with a wave of my hand.

Getting lost within the halls had helped clear my head a little, but how I managed to find halls without any windows to escape the building didn't help.

"Hey!" She smiled. "Where've you been?"

My face dropped. "Ask your brother."

"What did he do this time?" Her brows drew together.

"Don't worry about it." I waved off the question. I didn't feel like reliving it. It'd only piss me off again. "I'm starving and tired. That's all I care about right now."

"I can help you with that! Which do you want first, food or bed?"

My stomach growled. "Food."

Veron chuckled. "Follow me!"

Per usual, it was difficult to tell if I had been to this particular area of the castle or not. They should decorate the walls more. They could leave little seashell trails or have color themes.

These halls were busier than the others I'd swum through. Veron greeted every single merperson we passed by name, but it wasn't until one woman bent over in a coughing fit that Veron stopped.

The older mermaid hunched over and braced her hand against the wall. Her white-lavender hair hung in her face, and her shoulders shook with another round of coughing.

"Gloria, are you okay?" A worried crease formed on Veron's forehead as she rubbed the woman's back.

"Yes, dear. I'm fine," the mermaid wheezed.

Veron frowned. "You don't sound fine. How long has this been going on?"

Gloria straightened, giving Veron a kind smile. "It's just a cough, dear. Nothing to be concerned with."

Under her skin I could see a black tendril of veins peeking out from under her shirt and disappearing into a normal purple-blue color after a few inches.

Gloria noted my stare and readjusted her shirt before Veron noticed.

Veron watched her, and when the woman coughed again, she shook her head. "No. You need to go see someone."

"But your mother…" Gloria could barely finish the sentence. She patted her chest to help clear it.

"Whatever my mother wanted you to do, forget it. Go see a doctor. If this gets any worse, and you become bedridden, you will be unable to help your daughter care for your grandchildren. I'll pick up your duties for the day," Veron insisted.

"Don't be silly," Gloria chuckled.

"This isn't a debate. Go see a doctor. I will take care of your duties for the day."

Gloria searched Veron's face before hanging her head in defeat. "Yes, thank you."

Veron smiled in triumph. "Of course. Now off with you, and go get better. I'll speak with my mother later about what needs to be done."

Gloria bowed her head in gratitude before swimming off, her coughs echoing through the hall.

Veron sighed.

"Everything okay?"

Veron nodded. "Yeah, but that's the second mer this week I've sent to the doctor. I hope everything's okay."

"Maybe there's a cold going around," I said.

She raised an eyebrow. "A cold?"

"It's a common sickness for humans, although I assume there are different variants for different species. Usually, it causes someone to get a cough or runny nose, but nothing drastic. They get over it in a couple of days."

"I see. Let's hope it's only a cold then."

Veron turned right at the next hall, and at the very end, we came to an opening with a kitchen inside. Boulders and hardened sand served as tables, while rocks and shells had been turned into knives and other utensils. In the corner was a massive fireplace where the water from a hydrothermal vent shot upward. Along the wall surrounding the fire were white tubes, which a red bearded worm—a sedentary creature that lives in tubes and sustains a symbiotic relationship with microbes for survival—popped out of every few seconds.

I felt the heat from here.

"No one's here," I noted.

"It's in between meal times. Also, this is one of the smaller kitchens, and it's rarely used, which means it's always stocked," Veron explained. She went to work, grabbing strands of kelp, closed containers, and slices of fish hanging from re-used fishing hooks. The cool temperatures at this depth, mixed with the brine of the ocean, meant there was little risk of the food going bad.

"You're not scared of animals stealing the food?" I inquired.

Veron stifled her smile. "You can barely get around this castle. You really think an animal will find its way here?"

"Good point." I ran my fingers over the top of my tail, eyes trailing over the ingredients on the stone table. "Do you have something to help coagulate the ingredients together?"

Veron thought for a moment. "Yeah, I think ground sponge and fish egg could do the trick."

I smiled. "Great. Can I help?" I pretended to roll up my sleeves, which earned me an odd look from Veron.

"Sure." She shrugged.

I approached the table and grabbed a mortar and pestle sitting on the edge, one of the more recognizable items in the room. I threw in strips of kelp, and Veron passed me sponge and fish egg, which I added as well. I grinded it together until it became a paste. I carefully used slow hard strokes instead of quick ones, so the pieces wouldn't float away.

"More sponge!" I held out my hand, and Veron passed it to me.

"Should I cook up some fish?" she asked.

I nodded with a smile. "Yum! Yes!"

Veron shoved a long reed through two fish steaks, and placed them into the hydrothermal vent like she was cooking s'mores. Except she kept them in the boiling water for only about ten seconds.

"That was fast," I said.

My concoction had turned dough-like, and I kneaded it against the countertop.

Veron watched me with a tilt of her head, trying to make sense of what I was doing. "Yeah, the vents are extremely hot. It doesn't take long to completely cook something."

I split my kelp dough in half and handed it to Veron. "Flatten it as thinly as possible on the table, preferably in a rectangle."

We both got to work. Dough was more pliable under water than on land, but I still wished for a rolling pin.

"Done!" Veron grinned triumphantly at her work.

It definitely wasn't a rectangle, more like a blob. I bit my lip to hold back my laughter because she was so dang proud of herself.

"Great. Me too." I grabbed a sharp, knife-like shell and cut the dough into thin strips.

Veron copied my movements, and soon we had a pile of uncooked kelp pasta.

"Now what?" Veron asked.

I pointed to a mesh bag. "Can we use that to cook it?"

"Yup!" She snagged it off the wall and piled the strands inside. "How long?"

"Three seconds?"

Veron blinked at me.

Crap. They didn't use time the same as me.

"One, two, three." I counted my fingers until I held three in front of my face.

"I know how to count." Veron rolled her eyes.

Right, it was the seconds that she didn't understand.

"Two breaths," I corrected, hoping that was good enough.

She nodded, and three seconds later we had steaming pasta on the table.

We plated the pasta with the fish on top. When I took a bite, the fish melted in my mouth with a burst of briny goodness. The fish eggs added a smoky flavor.

"This is so good!" Veron exclaimed, eyeing her plate in surprise. "I had no idea this was going to be so good. What do you call it?"

"Pasta al pesce!" I said with a chef's kiss. Somehow, my chest both felt light and full.

Aunt Joan had taught me how to make pasta from scratch. She would be thrilled with this meal. She'd probably nitpick if she had made it, saying there wasn't enough balance, or it needed more acid.

Lemon would have been the perfect addition. But if I had made it, she would have done nothing but praised it.

I would love nothing more than to hear her gush over this dish, even knowing she could have made it better.

I had been writing down all her recipes, preparing to compile *Aunt Joan's Around the World Cookbook*. I had hoped it would inspire her to open a restaurant. But now it was one more thing I would never finish. I swallowed through my constricting throat. Would she go through my room? Clear it out and find it in my closet? Probably not, my parent's room was untouched, I had no doubt she'd leave mine that way too.

I shoved down the thoughts with another mouthful of pasta.

"Don't forget to drink water!" Veron tossed me a plastic water bottle she had taken from under the counter.

"I have to *drink* water? And from a plastic bottle!" I gaped as the clear container crinkled in my hands. "That's really weird. You'd think you wouldn't need to since you live in the water."

"Just like fish, our bodies get dehydrated because of being immersed in salt water. We have to drink to offset the osmosis, just like them. Colder, deeper water holds special nutrients we need too. But we can't live that deep, so groups of merpeople dive to collect the water." Veron took a swig from her own water bottle and gave a satisfied sigh. "We used to make weekly trips into the deep to drink, but since the amount of trash in the ocean has increased and plastic doesn't break down, we decided to use it to our advantage."

"The deep?" I snorted. "Like we aren't deep enough?" The water was dark all the time already. How much deeper did they need to go?

Veron smirked. "It's just what we call the deepest parts of the ocean, where we find the trenches."

I took a sip. It was cool and refreshing, reminding me of the crisp cucumber water I used to drink on a hot summer day. The perfect palate cleanser to our dish.

"Thanks for this," I said.

"I know this transition hasn't been easy." Veron ran her fingers through her blue-shaded hair. "I'm on your side. I do hope you can find peace here."

I stirred the makeshift fork through the food, losing my appetite. "I do too."

TWELVE

"What do you want to do today?" Veron asked with a little jump of excitement onto my bed.

I gave her a puzzled look. Aside from her, it's not like I had any warm welcomes. I figured having a low profile was the way to go.

"You're not a prisoner! We can have fun. It is my official duty to show you Oceanus and I think that should always start out with fun!"

"I don't know. What do you do for fun in Oceanus? If it's your official duty, then lead the way," I replied with a rush of nervous energy.

"We could swim through the garden, go to the market and shop, watch a game of finball, go to the sea horse grove…"

My favorite animals were seahorses, but I didn't have time to mention it because Veron was struck with an idea.

"Oh, I know! We can go check out a wreck! I know it may sound a little mundane to look at things from your own world. But wrecks are really cool, I promise. Also, I want to get Gavin a gift for standing up for you at the trial."

I scoffed. Yeah, he was doing a great job of standing up for me.

Veron stilled, becoming more serious than usual. "I talked to him about what happened yesterday. I think you misunderstood…"

"You weren't there," I cut in.

"No," she agreed. "But in his own way, he was trying to help. He's just pretty bad at it sometimes."

"Sure." I rolled my eyes.

She frowned. "I know Gavin can be hard to read, but he's a good guy."

"Guilty until proven innocent," I quoted.

"Isn't that exactly why you're upset? Because people are treating you that way? How can you turn around and do the same to my brother?"

I paused. I never thought of it like that before. Maybe I was being hypocritical, but I was exhausted from always needing to defend myself. "Except I haven't done anything wrong."

She sighed. "You should try talking to him. If you want everyone to understand things from your perspective, you should try to understand ours too. There are two sides to every story. Before you get upset, I agree he did a poor job with how he handled it, but his intentions were in the right place. Just talk to him," she encouraged.

"I'll think about it," I grumbled. But I had already thought about it. I knew I would end up talking to him eventually, I just didn't know when or how. Friendships weren't something I was well versed in anymore. I'd spent the last few years of my life being non-confrontational and avoidant. It would be uncomfortable to talk to him. But Veron was right. I needed to be an adult and hear his side, especially if I didn't have the full story like Veron insisted.

"Do you still want to go out?" Veron's hands twisted in her lap.

I smiled. "Of course."

I didn't want her thinking I was upset with her. Also, if I was no longer being avoidant, that meant I couldn't avoid finding my place within Oceanus too. Raiden told me to get out, meet people, and become a part of the community. Veron was encouraging the same thing. I needed to try.

"Is it okay if I invite some friends along?" Veron inquired.

"Yes, of course," I said. A great place to start was meeting more mers.

"Great. I'll meet you at the pearl gate in a bit. I'm going to go let them know."

"I'll head over when I'm done getting ready." Not that there was much to do. I couldn't change my clothes. But I could at least braid my hair to make it less unruly.

Veron left with a wave.

I turned a corner and groaned. I was lost. Again. In hindsight, I should have swum out of a window to the pearl gates. But I didn't want to get lost every time I left my room, and I thought finding the front entrance would have been easier after the past three weeks living here. In this place, one wrong turn was all it took.

One wrong turn had caused me to spend forty minutes swimming through dark gray passages lit by the tiny blue bioluminescent flecks. There were no windows leading out of the never-ending hallways.

My stomach churned. I hoped I wasn't near the creepy room from the other day.

I expected to run into another merperson and ask for directions, but hadn't seen a soul. Usually, the waters were filled with sounds of whales singing or fins flipping, but these halls were eerily quiet.

Voices finally echoed from up ahead.

It was Gavin—thank goodness. I crept up to a wooden door covered in barnacles and raised my hand to knock.

"Mom, this is becoming a serious problem," Gavin's voice strained to stay level.

"It's better for the merpeople to stay here in Oceanus where it's safe." Mirah's tone thumped through the water.

"But it won't be safe much longer! Dumping trash and killing ecosystems close to shore is already problematic, but the humans are getting closer to us!" Gavin's voice was no longer calm and collected.

"The chances of them continuing their path directly to Oceanus is very minimal. The ocean is a big place, and the current will surely push the fishing boats off their paths."

"What about the oil or waste dumps? There are currents that're pushing those destructive forces right toward us. Do you remember how much life died during the oil leak in the great gulf? This can't happen any longer."

"That's not our concern. We must do what's best for the merpeople."

Gavin's voice intensified. "Trying to stop them is what's best for the merpeople. Stopping the fisherman from discovering us or destroying any more habitats is the best course of action. The ocean isn't just for them or their food supply! We need the things they're taking too!"

"Son, it's better if we stay here. Together. All of us. If they end up near Oceanus, then we'll figure out what to do when the time comes," Mirah's voice stayed steady.

"We can't just figure it out when the time comes because then it will be too late. We have to start taking the initiative now. We have to save our home. Let me take some merpeople. I know many who would be willing to volunteer and who are ready to protect us and the beautiful places around us. Besides, the humans are only a few days out from the sea horses, and once they reach them, it could be detrimental for us."

"No, I'm sorry, but no. I cannot allow anyone to take such risks. We need to stick together. The humans have done a lot of harm to the oceans, but we've worked through such problems before. We've even learned to use some of their things to our advantage."

"I wouldn't call repurposing human garbage an advantage.

Please, Mother, let me do this." Gavin's voice shifted from anger to pleading.

"I said no."

"But they've already destroyed other—"

"Between the threat of the Abyssals and keeping the sickness under wraps, we have more pressing issues," she cut in.

"Is it a custom on land to listen in on conversations you haven't been invited to?"

I gasped with a startled sweep to my right.

"Speak, child." Councilman Jerod's baritone voice shook through my body.

"I'm...sorry. I got lost and was going to ask for help."

"How could any merperson get lost in the ocean?" The words cut through the waters making me flinch. "Such a pity." He looked me up and down.

I folded my arms over my bare skin.

"So this is what is destroying our ocean and putting us at risk. Pathetic," he spat.

Before I could respond, the barnacled door swung open.

"I knew I heard voices," Mirah said, looming in the doorway.

"Councilman Jerod, what're you doing here?" Gavin interjected from beside his mother.

I was tiny compared to the merpeople around me.

"I came to talk to your mother," Jerod side-eyed me, "about recent events, but ran into this one lurking outside the door"

Mirah glanced my way. "Ah, I see."

"I was on my way to meet Veron at the pearl gate, and I ended up getting lost. I was actually supposed to meet her earlier. I heard Gavin's voice and was going to ask him how to get there, but it seemed you were having an important conversation, and I didn't want to interrupt," I spewed in one breath.

Gavin covered his mouth to hide a smirk at my fumbling monologue.

I returned it with a glare before refocusing on Mirah and Jerod's imploring eyes.

"So, she just decided to listen instead," Jerod chimed in.

"I see," Mirah replied.

"Mom, I'm sure it's fine. I doubt she heard anything of importance," Gavin said, his gaze never leaving me.

"Besides the secrecy of the entire mer-realm, putting our entire livelihood at risk, and learning secrets that could expose us to the world?" Jerod barked.

"Why don't you show her the way out, Gavin, so Jerod and I can talk," Mirah calmly suggested.

"That'd be great," I said.

Gavin tilted his head in the direction of the empty hall. He gave his mother a slight bow and cast a piercing look at Jerod before leading us away.

We wandered through the halls in silence.

"Well, that wasn't intimidating." I broke the silence.

"You get used to it," Gavin noted.

"I know it's probably confidential, thus being discussed in the most secluded and creepy part of the castle, but is Oceanus really in so much danger?" My heart clenched at the thought of humans hurting a place I had already come to love so much.

No wonder they asked me all those questions.

"Billie—" Gavin paused, gave a deep sigh and continued. "Truthfully, the entire ocean is in danger."

"What do you mean?"

"That's exactly the danger. All the destruction is being caused by humans and none of you even realize it, because you don't have to live in it, and so, you don't think it's a big deal. But it is!"

"What? Us humans? You realize that not all humans are ripping up reefs and dumping trash!"

"But most humans are and there's very little action being taken to help stop it," Gavin fumed. "'How much damage can one human do?' is what everyone seems to think. Except that seems to be the singular mentality of billions of humans!"

"There are people doing things! I do things all the time! I almost died trying to save a sea turtle just a few days ago! You're the one who saved me, you saw me do that!" The water around me warmed. Gavin was being unfair, grouping all humans into the same category. And I was tired of having to defend myself, of defending an entire race. This kind of thinking is exactly what leads to holocausts. Why couldn't he just understand?

"Look, I know not all humans are terrible. If I thought that, I wouldn't have saved your life. But there's not enough action. Almost every day, I see the destruction or read reports of someone dying. You don't have to deal with it. I do! You may not have to deal with the repercussions right away, but we are."

"You and we, you and we. Stop separating us into the affected and unaffected or good versus evil!" I threw my braid over my shoulder.

"I'm not trying to. I just don't think humans understand the damage they're causing."

He didn't understand. It was so easy for him to group us into different categories instead of trying to understand we all live on this same planet, and we were all only trying to do our best. Maybe if they hadn't locked themselves away and hid from humanity, we'd be able to solve these problems together instead of just pointing fingers at us, at me, whenever something bad happened. Bubbles appeared on my skin where the water simmered.

Gavin released a sigh with a shake of his head. "I don't have the energy right now. I have too much to worry about."

My taut muscles relaxed, and my pursed lips turned into a concerned frown. Usually, Gavin was readily available to give me a run for my money, but this time, he really seemed exhausted. Veron had asked me to hear him out, maybe now was a good time. I could be a good listener.

I broke the silence. "It must be hard, trying to learn the ropes for the mer council."

"There's a lot happening with Oceanus, not all of it I agree with," he admitted.

"And did you agree with our 'talk'?"

His jaw ticked, and I worried that I had gone too far. "I didn't. Jerod insisted we get the information from you, and demanded that it be done in that way. He lost his wife to fishermen; she was caught in a trawling net same as you, but she wasn't so lucky. She was crushed before being rescued and he had to drag her from the net himself to avoid discovery. Apparently, she was fairly mutilated by that point. What's worse, his son was there. I think it really affected them both."

"That's terrible," I uttered. And I meant it.

"A lot of us have similar stories. That's why we don't have the nicest things to say about humans. I was worried he'd try to somehow avenge his wife's death if he was alone in the room with you. I don't think he'd outright kill you, but I don't trust him either. My mom wouldn't listen, so I insisted on being the one to interrogate you." His eyes darted to mine. "I am sorry about how it occurred. They gave me a script to follow. I just figured it was better for it to be me than anyone else."

I held his gaze this time.

Veron was right. He had been trying to protect me, but I was too stubborn to see it. Clearly, he held contempt for humans like many mers, and for good reason, but since the beginning he had done nothing but try to help me. If he could put his feelings aside, I could return the kindness.

I cocked my head to the side. "You should come with us."

His eyebrow arced up. "What do you mean?"

"Come with me, Veron, and her friends to a shipwreck. If they're still waiting by the time we get to the gate. It'll be fun! Come enjoy this ocean you're hell-bent on protecting from me and my kind," I prodded him.

Gavin scratched the side of his head. "All right, yeah. Let's go."

THIRTEEN

"Where have you been?" Veron screeched.

I jerked my tail to propel myself forward. "I'm so sorry," I said. I hadn't expected them to still be here and guilt settled in my abdomen about making them wait. After my parents died, I was notoriously late anytime I actually bothered to go hang out with my friends, and this led to me losing them. I didn't want to repeat the past.

"Don't blame her. I held her up. We ran into Mother and Jerod. And, of course, Jerod needed to intimidate the human," Gavin said.

"She doesn't look very human to me." A mermaid cocked one eyebrow. Her hair was a deep green, reminding me of kelp forests.

"Yeah, currently I do seem to be in that predicament." I attempted to lighten the mood with a soft smile at the girl. "I'm Billie."

"I don't know who would want to be human. Being a mermaid is magical and wondrous." Another mermaid next to Veron gave a backward flip in the water, brushing the face of the third unknown mermaid with her iridescent yellow tail.

"Hey! Laurelina, keep it to yourself." The third mermaid batted away the second mermaid's tail. Her own tail was nearly black, along with her hair pulled into a fishtail braid that went to her waist.

"Ashmay, you know Laurelina is too sweet and finds everything magical. I think it's literally impossible for her to keep it to herself." The green tinted mermaid chimed into the banter.

The three of them eyed each other before bursting into childish giggles.

"Just ignore them." Veron flipped her hand at her friends.

"Oh no. Don't worry about it." I gleamed. Their boisterous energy was infectious, and it was nice to have some lighthearted banter again.

Gavin cleared his throat next to me, and the three mermaids sobered.

"Sorry, Gavin," the yellow-tailed mermaid said.

"He's fine. And that was directed to me not you," Veron voiced. "He was trying to, unsubtly I might add, get me to introduce everyone. So that's Laurelina, Ashmay, and Lillet." Veron pointed first to the girl with the yellow tail, then to the girl with the black tail and hair, and finally to the girl with the green hair.

"Nice to meet all of you," I said. "Do you all know each other from school?"

"School? What's school?" Lillet arched her eyebrows, which framed her facial features.

"Oh my gosh, Lillet! Don't be such a pacha," Ashmay hissed. "She knows what school is. We don't have a formal setting here. There isn't enough room to dedicate a building to all the merkids, so we are homeschooled."

"What's a pacha?" I asked, moving on from Lillet's ribbing. "And how does everyone know so much about the human world?" It had been a question I was dying to ask, but assumed it was due to the ranking of the other mers I had met. Observing how much other mermaids knew about my world took me by surprise.

"Pacha is mer-slang for the word pain. It can either be used to describe an actual pain or to tell someone they're being one,"

Ashmay explained.

"And it's our job to understand humans. It's our best way of staying safe," Veron added.

Gavin rolled his eyes at the quartet.

"No need to be such a downer, Gavin. Come on, perk up! We have adventures ahead of us," Laurelina chimed.

"Speaking of which, we should head off to the sinking before it gets too dark. Are you coming, Gavin?" Veron's face grew serious, blocking any emotions from displaying on her face.

Ah, they truly were siblings. I knew Gavin was well versed in this, but I didn't realize it was a trick Veron could so easily do too.

"If you don't mind," Gavin said.

"I'm sorry. I invited him. I didn't think it'd be a problem. I hope it's not." A knot began to form in my stomach.

"Not at all. It'll be fun," Lillet said.

"Everyone knows Gavin can use a little more fun in his life," Ashmay mocked. "He's such a womble."

The girls burst into a fit of giggles as Gavin floated beside me glaring at them.

Feeling lost, I wrung my hands in silence.

"Now if that isn't true, I don't know what is," Veron agreed as she saw my perplexed face. "Womble means… It's a way to mock someone who takes everything too seriously. Maybe worrywart is a better way to describe it."

"Okay, that's enough of you four. Let's get going." Gavin swam up and over the mermaids, leaving me to hover in his wake.

They took off after him, and the pressure from the momentum of all their tails propelled me away.

I rubbed the flurrying sand from my eyes, and striking my tail in the direction of the dust storm, I pushed the grains the other way and pursued the group.

We rose higher into the water column so the bottom wouldn't stir, and eventually Veron slowed her pace to linger in the back with me.

"I'm really surprised you got him to come along. What'd it take?" Veron whispered so the water wouldn't carry our conversation.

"What do you mean?" I matched her decibel.

"Gavin has always had this insurmountable sense of higher duty. I remember when we were little, we used to have so much fun. He'd often play games with me, take me to hidden caves, and show me endangered species that were rarely seen. But as we grew up, it stopped. I don't really know why, but he changed. He's no longer the fun-loving older brother he once was. He's always so serious. I've been trying to get him to go to shipwrecks with all of us for years now, but all he ever says is how he has more important things to worry about." Veron meticulously watched the ground as the water around her grew chilly.

"Really? I know he's rather serious, but it didn't take much to convince him to come along. I simply asked." I reached over and squeezed her arm.

"Whatever the reason, thanks." Veron fell quiet. She had a far off look in her eyes, as though lost in her thoughts.

I admired how astute Veron was. Most humans I knew didn't pay attention to others' problems or what was happening around them. They were too busy being wrapped up in themselves. I wasn't criticizing. I'm like that too. Granted, I matured faster than most people my age after my parents died, but I never gave a second thought to my classmates' wellbeing. And I only occasionally wondered how my aunt felt after losing her sister. Veron was much more mature.

The group was silent as we swam through the ocean. Nothing but the soft swish of our tails revealed our location.

Tiny crackles of shrimp clicked their claws together, reminding me of when I'd fill my mouth with a handful of Pop Rocks.

A manta ray glided through the waters barely within visibility. It displayed the unique markings on its stomach when it took a sharp turn to circle back around. Its dark wings flapped effortlessly, propelling itself.

It was so calming. There was no rush to its movements or need to get anywhere quickly. It was peaceful with life, living in the moment, and seemed content with the waters that surrounded it. Gliding through the waters, gliding through life.

I closed my eyes as I swam, breathing deeply.

The cool, salty water entered my nose, taking with it all the fears, problems, and concerns of the moment. In this moment, I could just be. I felt the water rush past my smooth skin and scales, heard the sweet melodic sounds of cetaceans, and focused on being in the moment. It isn't every day that a person gets to experience the life of a mermaid.

When I opened my eyes, no one was in front of me anymore. I swore I had heard their tails and breaths while swimming.

I slowed.

"Tired already?" A playful voice joked as a mermaid with deep maroon hair and a red-orange tail swam by.

My jaw dropped in awe of the melding of the reds to oranges and back again on Ashmay's tail. It was as if Georgia O'Keeffe had painted the tail by hand. I hadn't realized how much higher we had swum.

Ashmay's tail and hair had only appeared dark because the palace was so deep below the water's surface. The red and orange light spectrums couldn't penetrate that far.

"Your tail is amazing!" I swooned.

"Thanks. I'm sad that I don't get to show it off too often with Oceanus at such low elevation. But it's great for getting water."

I tilted my head. "What does that have to do with the color of your hair and tail?"

"The deep ocean has a lot of weird and unknown creatures. It's hard for us to see down there and it can get dangerous. Since these colors don't penetrate that far in the water, red basically makes you invisible to them." Ashmay laughed at my gaping face. "Most merpeople have to paint themselves red to help them disappear. My parents don't like me collecting deep sea water, but since I don't have to add on a lot of extra color, they usually let me help out. We all have to lend a hand however we can."

"That's so cool! I want to go! Can I help sometime?" I exclaimed.

"Slow down, tiger shark. Maybe you should learn to swim with your fin before going to the deep." Lillet filled in on my left.

"Yeah, I guess. But I'm not that bad. I used to be on my school's swim team." Despite my argument, we all knew I was nowhere near the same level as them.

They glided through the waters without looking ahead and breathed as if they had gone for a short stroll. Meanwhile, I had to constantly watch the ground to make sure I wasn't sinking down or floating up. My breath sounded like I had run a few miles.

"Fine, fine. I'll wait." I pouted.

"We're here!" Veron yelped.

I peered into the sandy valley below.

A freighter ship filled the basin with leftover cargo boxes being taken over by blue, green, and red algae. When Veron mentioned a shipwreck, I had expected an old schooner with rotting wood, filled with hidden treasures. I didn't expect to look down on a massive modern day cargo ship made out of metal.

"That's it?" I frowned.

"What do you mean that's it? I bet we can find some really nifty things in those metal boxes," Veron rebutted.

"I expected a real ship. This is boring and so...*modern*," I huffed.

"All the old ships have been excavated or are used by scuba divers. You'd be surprised how many little ships end up down here after hurricanes. This ship is my favorite place to find things because it's so big that I find something new every time." Veron gave me a little nudge with her elbow. "Oh, come on. Sorry it isn't what you had in mind."

I narrowed my eyes at her, which was met with delighted bright violet eyes. How could anyone deny Veron with that look? "This better be good," I grumbled.

Everyone swam down the sand bank and soon the ship loomed over us. It was gigantic from above, but I hadn't comprehended the extent of the impending mass until we had swum closer. To think hurricanes could take down something of this size was baffling.

We swam along the side of it.

Purple circles with diameters of one to two feet decorated the side. I swam past a bright purple patch and a sergeant major fish darted in my direction.

Its usual color was a yellow dorsal turning to silver at its belly with thick black stripes tracing vertically down the body. When the fish swam close to me, the entire thing turned stark black.

My eyes widened as the fish transformed before me. I stopped swimming, and watched it grow darker as it moved closer.

"Ow! What the—" I grasped my arm where the fish nipped me.

"Are you okay?" Gavin called from above.

"Yeah. It didn't actually hurt. Sorry. It surprised me." I let out a short laugh while eyeing the fish nervously.

"Get away from the nest. You're too close." Gavin shook his head.

"What?" I questioned as I swam closer to him.

"I said, you were too close. Sergeant majors are really territorial, especially when it comes to their eggs. When they change colors, it means they're on the defensive. Typically, when something changes color in the ocean, there's a reason for it," Gavin explained.

"That's so cool!" I stared down at the purple nests. Each one was guarded by multiple fish.

"It's cool because they're small and harmless. It's less cool with other creatures," Gavin said.

A shudder ran through me. I had no desire to meet the 'less cool' creatures.

Meandering inside to the bridge, I ran my hands over knobs, handles, and buttons. Nothing lit up since the electrical wiring had been destroyed by the water. My breath shortened when my eyes veered over to a CD player—music.

It's been forever since I heard music! At least, that's what it felt like for someone who used to listen to music every single day. I ran my finger over the black plastic, twisting the volume up and watched the darkened red power light. I closed my eyes and imagined the tunes of Rosemary Clooney, Ray Charles, Led Zeppelin, Queen, and all my beloved classics.

I missed home.

A short, amused snort escaped me. Missing land more than the ocean, that was a first for me. But it was true. And I worried about Aunt Joan.

She must have tried to get the entire coast guard to look for me. I hoped she was okay, not putting her life on pause. She'd already spent the last four years doing that for me. It seemed to be her own personal promise to my mom, and I imagined she felt like she had failed. She had given up everything for me, and I returned nothing, and now she probably thought I was dead. I can only imagine how heartbroken she must be.

If heaven was real, and my parents could see me, I wonder if that's how they felt for the first couple of years. I hated the idea of them watching me lose my friends, turn mute, and receive poor grades.

The water around me grew brisk, sending a shiver to the tip of my tail.

A clang through the water jolted me back to the present.

"Everything okay out here?" I popped my head outside and saw Veron flinging things out of the cargo ship.

"No! I can't find anything! This totally sucks. All the containers are just filled with meaningless crap," Veron bellyached.

"What did you find?" I wondered, hoping to bring back her positivity.

"Just that junk." Veron glared over her shoulder at all the random artifacts strewn along the ground.

I swam over to the items. They did seem rather meaningless, mostly torn rags or pieces of mechanical parts. Nothing seemed intact or exciting, but something glinted from underneath a brown cloth.

"Was this in the container?" I exclaimed.

"The weird circle? I don't know. It seems like junk to me. Who cares where they came from?" Veron turned away, unenthused with what I held.

I squeezed the wooden circle. It was covered in cloth and metal circles lining the outside. When I shook it, a shimmering metallic clatter resounded through the water. I gave the cloth a hard thunk and my hand bounced off it perfectly.

I was holding an intact tambourine; the easiest of the instruments to play. My heartbeat quickened, and my stomach twisted as I tapped the cloth, giving it a little shake. I bit my bottom lip in anticipation.

Peering over my right shoulder, the rest of the gang was busy, and no one was paying attention. I turned back, raised my hands, cleared my mind, and let go.

FOURTEEN

The water filled with the bongs, clinks, tings, and thumps as I created a basic beat with the tambourine. My lips opened to sing the music I missed so much. The songs my mother used to play in the morning and the ones I would listen to after coming home from school. I grinned as adrenaline coursed through my veins, lighting me up from the inside out.

Closing my eyes, Bob Dylan's *Thunder On The Mountain* flew from my lips, surrounding me with their melody.

"What're you doing?" Laurelina interjected.

I jumped, clutching the tambourine to my chest to silence it. "Sorry. I was playing some music. I guess I got a little carried away."

"What's a twister?" Veron swam up behind Laurelina, no longer furiously flinging things around.

I hesitated, unsure how I could describe a tornado. "During a storm, sometimes the winds get so strong that they spin quickly and destroy everything in their path."

"Like a hurricane?" Ashmay appeared over the side.

"Kind of, but a lot smaller, and on land. They're a lot more unpredictable," I added.

"Have you ever seen a mountain?" Veron clapped her hands

excitedly.

"Sure." I shrugged.

Veron's eyes became as big as saucers, "What're they like?"

Everyone leaned in.

I quashed my smile before answering. "Imagine a rock as a trench, but goes straight into the air, above the clouds, and can go on for hundreds or thousands of miles. Sometimes there can be snow on them and they are filled with trees and wild animals." Watching everyone's eyes and mouths widen with each word had me chuckling.

"Can you play more?" Lillet chimed in.

"I guess you don't know everything about land," I teased.

"We only know what we've heard from stories that other merpeople tell. We don't have many personal experiences because going to the surface is forbidden for our safety, so even those who know new things won't speak about them in fear of someone learning they broke the rule," Gavin explained, watching from behind everyone.

"I once listened to human music from under the water, the thumping from the music could be heard one hundred feet down, but I couldn't make out the words." Ashmay thrust her chest out in pride.

"You what?" Veron looked at her wide eyed. "Wow, I'm so jealous," she squealed with a twirl in the water.

Gavin eyed his sister disapprovingly, causing her to slink back down.

"You're singing rivals the most beautiful whale song," Veron said.

I blushed. "Music with words that touch your soul is one of the greatest things ever made. Let me teach you a few things about my world for once." I broke out with a basic beat, watching as everyone eyed my actions with the utmost interest. I waited a few beats more before breaking into the melodic tunes of The Cranberries.

I changed to a more upbeat song, and grinned when Ashmay

started to sway and bounce to the music.

Next thing I knew, all the mermaids had broken out into a dance. They twirled, flipped, spun, shook their tails, waved their hands, and Lillet even started to sing along during the chorus.

Gavin stood off to the side and watched the menagerie of music and dancing with crossed arms.

Laurelina swam over to him, grabbed his arm, unfolding his harsh stature, and brought him into the middle. She held both hands and pulled them back and forth, forcing his body to move to and fro.

Gavin swayed with an unamused face for a few seconds before he raised his hand and twirled her around.

A giggle escaped Laurelina's lips, and he responded with a beaming smile. He swam between the girls, taking a turn with each of them to whirl them in a dancing frenzy.

Veron's eyes twinkled at her brother, catching his eye, and he swept her up into his arms. He spun her around and brought her down into a tranquil dip.

Veron broke away with a squeal of delight.

Everyone continued with their acrobatic dancing through the weightless water.

"That was amazing!" Veron cheered at me when the song ended. "Can you teach me?"

"That may have to be saved for another time. It's starting to get dark." Gavin's usual cold demeanor returned.

"Oh come on, just a little bit longer. You were having fun too," I pressed.

"No, it's getting dark and there're too many of us to try and find our way back. None of you are trained for night travel and could easily get lost." Gavin crossed his arms over his chest, straightening his stature.

"We did fine when you first took me to Oceanus as your captive. And now we don't have to worry about anyone trying to run away," I prodded.

"No. You don't know these waters and your ignorance of this is going to cause us trouble. Now please stop this absurdity of thinking you know everything," Gavin sneered.

"Thinking I know everything? Speak for yourself! It's not like you're any more of an adult than the rest of us." I couldn't believe his stubbornness.

"Well, then, don't act like a child. Do you think I like having to be the adult? No. I'm not your parents, Billie. I don't want to have to look after everyone." Gavin pursed his lips.

My hand clenched around the tambourine. "No, you're not and I don't expect you to be. I'm pretty used to being on my own since my parents are dead." I dropped the tambourine, turned away, and began swimming back toward Oceanus with Veron following close behind me.

Ψ

I sat at the edge of Veron's bed. I mostly hung off the edge, but I used my tail to keep from falling off completely. My back was stiff as I gazed down at my fingers, picking at my flimsy nails.

The salt water was not conducive to long fingernails, making them brittle and easy to pick away.

"I'm sorry he said that," Veron said as she sat beside me.

My entire body stiffened. I did everything possible to hold myself together, but the comfort of someone made me want to collapse. I took a deep breath. I'd be back in my room soon. The only reason I had accepted Veron's request to go to her room was so she didn't think I was bothered by Gavin's comment, not because I wanted to talk about what happened.

"No, really, it's fine. I'm tired," I lied with a tight smile.

"Are you sure?" Veron rubbed my back.

The lump in my throat stopped my response. I wouldn't cry. I wouldn't give in. My parents were gone, and I had dealt with it. Crying wouldn't bring them back; it would only bring pity from others. And I really didn't want to deal with their pity. I just wanted to be by myself.

"Veron, I'm gonna go. It's been a long day and I'm not used to swimming around as much as everyone else. I'm pooped. Thanks for worrying though. You're a total sweetheart and it means a lot to me," I said. I meant every word.

I adored that Veron cared, but I already owed her so much. I didn't need her or anyone. I was used to dealing with things by myself.

"If you need anything, please let me know," Veron said. "And thanks again for convincing Gavin to have some fun, even if it didn't end so well." Veron chewed the inside of her cheek as her green painted tail flicked anxiously across the ground.

"Of course. It's the least I could do for everything you've done. You saved my life. I would do a whole lot more for you than just get your stinking brother to loosen up."

Veron's face lit up, and I was relieved she was finally letting go of her worry.

"Goodnight. Don't go getting lost now." Veron stuck out her tongue with a wink.

"Ruin all my fun," I joked.

We gave each other a quick hug before I headed out into the hall.

I drifted along, listening to the muted waters. All I heard was the soft swishing of my tail. I twisted and turned through the grayish blue halls, my thoughts meandering aimlessly as well.

I thought of my parents, wondered how my aunt was doing, if Veron was upset with me for fighting with Gavin, why Gavin acted the way he did, what Gavin and Mirah had talked about, what I would do if I couldn't turn human again, and all the endless questions I had. Did I even want to go back to my old life? To my solitary life on land? It seemed my life in the water would mimic that way of life. But at least on land, I had Aunt Joan. I knew she gave up a lot to take care of me, and I had always felt it was my fault that my aunt didn't pursue her dreams, but I still missed her.

Here, there was the prospect of friends. I couldn't remember the last time I had laughed with people my own age. I didn't know what life I'd choose, but it's not as if I had a choice.

When I opened my bedroom door, I noticed a figure sitting in a chair in the dark corner, staring at me.

I stood in the doorway, unable to move. Fear held me. The figure got up from the chair and moved forward into the light.

"I didn't mean to scare you." Mirah's plum-colored tail swayed gracefully with long strands of her silvery-green hair floating behind her.

"Do you often hide in other people's rooms?" I huffed.

Mirah raised her eyebrows. "You really are a feisty human, aren't you?"

"I'm not human," I retorted.

"Oh?"

"I mean, I am," I hesitated. "I am human. Just not now. I'm not human right now. I'm feisty in general."

"I'll give you that."

I shifted in the doorway, catching a fruity smell in the water as Mirah moved toward me.

"I came here because I wanted to tell you that I'm sorry for earlier today. I didn't mean to come off so harsh and unyielding; however, we do seem to have that in common. I hope that I didn't make you feel unwelcome, and if I did, I would like to correct that mistake," Mirah explained.

I glided over to the bed and floated down. "I hope you know that it's never been my intention to intrude or be a burden. I'm trying to figure everything out too."

"It seems you've been put into quite a surprising predicament.

It's very understandable." Mirah loomed over me now, blocking out the light so she was nothing but dark shadow.

"You can sit down if you'd like," I offered.

"Thank you." Mirah's features reappeared as she sat, and I saw a rare, soft smile. We sat in silence for a few minutes, probably both thinking of what to say next.

"Is what you and Gavin were talking about a big problem?" I blurted out.

Silence.

"There are a lot of problems going on in the ocean that most don't know about." Mirah's face fell.

"But is it a big problem? Gavin made it sound like it's a large predicament, but you brushed him off. I know there are problems, but is it really that bad?" My brows furrowed as the ache in my chest returned.

"In short, yes. I'm not going to sugarcoat anything for you, Billie. There are many atrocities happening in the ocean right now, and we merpeople can only do so much." Mirah glanced down at my black-streaked, blue tail.

Silence.

"What can be done?" I asked.

"Stop discarding waste in our waters, stop trawling our ecosystems, stop oils and pesticides from leaking into our waters, stop destroying mangroves which are the nurseries of our fish, stop moving species across the globe and making them invasive in new areas, there is so much that needs to stop, too much. Even the destruction caused by natural forces, like hurricanes, is treacherous, and they're getting stronger as the waters grow warmer."

Silence.

"Right now, we can focus on the fishermen not finding Oceanus. I've been taking merpeople out to try and direct the fish in order to redirect the boats, but they keep heading this way. All we can do is handle one thing at a time. Aside from that, what can we do?"

I nodded. "Yeah, I guess it's not like you can swim up to a human and ask them to stop." I almost wanted to laugh at the thought of a person being startled by a mermaid popping out of the water. But I didn't.

"I suppose not," Mirah responded.

Silence.

"Didn't someone say humans only get turned into mermaids if there's a purpose?" I queried.

"From what we understand, yes."

"Do you think this was my purpose? To learn about this on a firsthand basis, hear it from merpeople, and be able to take the message to land in a way you cannot." My voice grew louder as I continued, "Do you think my reason for becoming a mermaid is to hear your voices and go back to land to stand up against this?"

"It's definitely a possibility." Mirah smiled and patted my fin. "I'm glad you're on our side. You have a lot of spunk."

I smirked at hearing Mirah use the word spunk. I was glad I had a place, a purpose, and that I had spunk.

"I should get going. You've had a long day and I need to think some things through." Mirah got up from the bed and crossed the room to the door.

"Mirah?"

"Yes?" She turned her stormy gray eyes on me.

"I'm glad I became a mermaid."

Mirah paused at the door. "I'm glad to hear that, but please be careful. Not everyone feels the same way. Yes, the mer council allowed you to live among us, but that does not mean it was unanimous." Without waiting for a response, she left.

Silence.

FIFTEEN

"*Mommy! Mommy! I had a bad dream!*" *My wide-eyed, five-year-old self jumped into my parents' bed.*

"*Huh? What is it sweetie?*" *My mom groggily replied, scooping me into a cuddle.*

I sniffled, "I had a bad dream. There was a bad man with orange eyes in the ocean. I was making a sandcastle. Gobo ran into the water to chase a bird, and the mean man pulled Gobo under the water." I cried as our rescued Jack Russell mutt popped his head up from the end of the bed at the sound of his name.

"*Oh, honey, it was just a nightmare. See? Gobo is fine.*" *My mom pointed to the dog who crept forward to lick my salty cheek.*

I giggled, wrapping my arms around him.

"*Everything okay?*" *My dad breathed out between snores.*

"*It's fine, keep sleeping, sweetie.*" *Mom and I sniggered together.*

"*I'm scared to sleep, Mommy. What if he comes back?*" *I burrowed my face into Gobo's fur.*

Mom replied by simply humming a light song. Music always made me feel better. I drifted back to sleep with Gobo beside me and my mother's arm wrapped around us both.

Orange eyes.

My eyes flew open. A shiver ran through my body. I had forgotten about the orange-eyed man. Dreams with him and his eyes had haunted me for years when I was a kid. But as I grew up, both the fears and the memories disappeared. I peered around my cream-colored room, my senses dampening as claustrophobia set in.

After my conversation with Mirah, it had been suggested to Gavin that I should lay low for a few days. Mirah had assured Gavin that she would inform him when it was safe for me to leave the palace. That was a week ago.

I had become a disease that could spread like wildfire through Oceanus, and it seemed safer to keep the contagion (me) locked up. I no longer got lost among the palace halls that had once filled me with awe, but meandered through them in a sleepy haze. I knew there were eleven kitchens, eighty-three bedrooms, twenty-two common rooms, forty-nine closets, and nineteen unknown rooms. This brilliant palace was now nothing more than a sandcastle I wished a tide would sweep away. At least then I'd have some freedom.

Veron did a good job of keeping me entertained, bringing me books from two libraries written by mer authors. I was flabbergasted to learn they had found a way to use squid ink to write underwater on algae-pressed paper. Even though Veron had tried to explain the process, the underwater science behind the creation of the paper and the emulsification of the stringy ink so they bonded was beyond my understanding.

I read merpeople folklore and the first constitution of the establishment of Oceanus. I even read a book on Oceanus's family trees.

For some reason, I searched for my parents' names. I couldn't help but wonder if my parents had been saved the same way as me. But no matter how much material I searched through, there was no account of an incident like mine. There wasn't a single account of a human turning into a mermaid. It only seemed to exist in the minds of the mers, and as nothing more than a bedtime story, which appeared to be exactly how they wanted to keep it.

Veron told me about a poem Gavin had recited to her when she was younger, and went to the libraries looking for it. She swore it had something to do with change, but kept coming up empty.

Gavin occasionally bumped into me on his way to do his mother's bidding. Every time I saw him, he had a sour look on his face. Whether he was disgusted by my presence or something else was a mystery. I tried asking what was bothering him, but was met with a dismissal; there was always something important he had to take care of. After a couple of weeks, I learned to stop asking questions.

I heaved a sigh at the same brown-swirled shell on the ceiling above my bed. It was a shell I had stared at for the past two hours, trying to figure out how to avoid going mentally insane.

I left the bed with a flick of my tail and moved to the window.

Peering outside, I could see everyone bustling in the streets below—chatting, musing, and working. I wouldn't have considered myself a productive person, but I couldn't handle being locked away a moment longer.

"Screw this," I said. I wasn't going to sit anymore, waiting until the great and powerful Mirah gave me permission to not be an abomination on her land. That day would probably never come, but even if it did, I wasn't about to wait around for it.

I ripped the seaweed to the side, lay my hands on the grainy sill, and with a little thrust, pulled myself outside.

The fresh water from the current swept across me, giving me new life. I smiled, no longer in stagnant water. Finally, the weight of the sand from the castle lifted off my chest.

Ready or not, Oceanus, here I come.

I swam to the city streets below. Vast volumes of merpeople skirted around me as I swam right to the center of town, and it was like I had landed in the middle of a street fair.

Merchildren played tag above their shopping parents. Every

once in a while, they'd lose their bearing and tumble down onto the merpeople beneath. The parents frantically pulled their children off strangers' heads, forcing the children to apologize profusely before rejoining the menagerie.

Merpeople tousled me, but to my surprise, no one gave me a second look. If anyone knew who I was, they made no allusion to it. Instead, they filled their bags with sponges, clumps of seaweed, pebbles, bottled water, and any other necessary items.

"I have fresh squid brought from the tropics of the Red Sea. It's only fifteen globus, best deal in the sea, guaranteed!" A gaunt, old merman shoved a plaque-white, diamond headed fish in my face. He gave me a toothy grin, waiting for me to succumb to his offerings.

"I'm sorry. I'm just browsing." I didn't know their currency. In the weeks I had been here, I had never seen people buying anything. I had assumed the merpeople got what they needed from friends or themselves. I guess I had imagined an older hunter-gatherer motif.

"Well, these parts aren't for browsin'. If you wanted to go for a swim, go somewhere else." The old man slammed the squid back on the rock table where an array of shells, fish, algae, and other concoctions resided.

I scowled at the old man before moseying on. Even if I did have money, I wouldn't buy from him.

It surprised me; everyone I'd met in the palace conducted themselves responsibly, almost with a posh mannerism. I wouldn't go as far as to say they were snobbish, but close. Here in the market, everyone haggled, bantered, and rarely said sorry when bumping into another merperson. It wasn't a place for those faint of heart, and elbows were definitely put to use. It was much more obnoxious...rude...human? I could have been in New York City rather than thousands of feet underwater.

Eventually, I got bored of window shopping and I didn't need any more bruises. I skidded around a larger mermaid who balanced a dead brain coral on top of her head. The coral was white and easily the same size as the woman.

I entered an empty alley and let out a sigh of relief to get away from the crowds.

I swam through the random streets. They curved, intersected, and branched off into smaller streets, making me think of the pictures of Venice my aunt had shown me.

I admired the architecture of the stone and sand buildings looming around me. They were solid structures as though each sand granule had been placed in a very particular spot. Despite being built of wet sand and rock, they felt as sturdy as brick.

On some of the buildings sat carved gargoyles. Unlike those on land, these gargoyles represented sea creatures—dolphins, octopods, seals, crabs, and nudibranchs. There were statues of unknown sea animals too. Fish and creatures of nightmares rather than the ocean creatures I had come to know and love. They stared at me with giant, soulless eyes and massive teeth carved so sharp I didn't dare touch them for fear they would prick my finger.

Who would choose to put something so terrifying on their house? There was no way I was sticking around to find out firsthand.

I turned down another alley, another street, another corner, and so on. Swimming for nearly two hours, I rarely ran into anyone since they were all near the main market.

The twists and turns dizzied me. I turned yet another corner. Staring at the ground, I tried to steady myself. I looked up for a second before slamming into a wall.

Another dead end.

I leaned my head against the wall and took a centering breath. I needed rest. I should head back to the castle before anyone realized I was missing. Veron would freak out if she couldn't find me, and no one knew I was here.

I took another deep breath.

Vertigo was easy to come by in the ocean, especially for a human, er, ex-human.

"Look what we have here. If it isn't the land princess herself," a young male voice sneered from behind.

The water grew cold around me, electrifying to the point of pain.

I went rigid, and my eyes shot open.

"She's kinda cute, don't ya think?"

My heart hammered against my chest.

Above me, drifted another merman with long dark hair floating around his face, shadowing his features. I could see his wide grin protruding from the darkness. I felt like a gazelle looking at a lion.

"Look at her tan skin. It's like a delicacy. 'The best deal in the sea, guaranteed!'" A third voice mocked.

I turned, putting my back against the wall.

Five mermen surrounded me, grinning. They looked to be in their twenties and were all larger than me.

I needed to get out of this alley. I was nothing more than a mouse caught in a trap, however, there was enough distance between the three who swam in front of me and the two above me, I might be able to slip between the two distinct groups. I wouldn't give them the satisfaction of responding. I'd just leave.

I thrust my tail and beelined through the opening toward the top of the buildings. Too slow.

Rough arms reached around my tail and flung me back down to the ground.

When had they spread out and blocked the gap? There was no longer any way for me to escape.

"Baby, why're you trying to swim away? We just want to welcome you," the merman said, floating directly in front of me.

"Don't call me baby," I spat back.

"I'll call you whatever I want, sweet cheeks." His shadowed face came closer as he swam toward me. He stopped a foot away.

His gray eyes pierced through me like a rusted blade.

I refused to look away despite the fear coursing through my veins. Each time my heart pulsed, it sent an electric shock through my body.

His hands reached forward and lightly touched my right cheek, leaving an icy trail. "You're one of them, huh? The ones who poisoned my uncle with oil wastelands, slowly killing him. And your seismic blasts...don't even get me started on the mass murders you commit when you test your explosions in the water." His eyes narrowed. He moved his hand down to my shoulder and dug his sharp fingernails into my skin, piercing me.

I bit down on my tongue to stop myself from crying out. I wouldn't show weakness.

His blood orange tail pushed my tail into the ground. He was above me now, his whole body weight holding me in place. He snarled, eyeing my neck like he planned to rip out my throat.

I clenched my hands and pushed against the ground. I wouldn't hang my head in shame. "It wasn't me."

"Excuse me?" His claws dug deeper.

"I didn't do those things." I kept my voice from cracking despite the exhaustion and pain coursing through my body. His strength weakened me.

"Maybe you didn't, but you humans are all the same. You don't care about anything else but yourselves."

"That's not true. I'm sorry you feel that way, but it's just not true. I care about the ocean. I want to help the ocean, and there are plenty of other people in the world also doing what they can to help. Trying to spread awareness, to make a difference, and to reverse the destruction that has occurred. It's possible to change things if we work together, and I only know this because of other humans who've told me we can fix this, like my parents." Tears brimmed in my eyes. It was an odd sensation. I only knew they were there because the budding droplets had a different glimmer than the surrounding water. It was like seeing the air just above the heated black top.

"Well, apparently not enough of you care because I haven't seen much of a difference."

"Well, you won't if you don't try opening your eyes to it." I was irritated now. How dare he judge me and say I don't care? How dare he make these assumptions without knowing anything about me? How dare he assault me physically and verbally?

He pushed harder.

"Will you get off me?" I garbled through clenched teeth.

"What do you want, baby? Can't you ask nicely?" He smirked down at me as a strand of slick black hair fell in front of his steely gaze.

"I said, get off. Of. Me," I snapped.

"Maybe if you say please..." The guy's eyes sparkled as his friends chuckled around him.

"You heard her. She said, get off!" A melodic voice came from above.

The boy's hand was yanked off my shoulder as he was flung through the water.

SIXTEEN

Relief rushed through my body as the pressure subsided. I stole a calming breath and pushed myself up from the ground.

My tail was strewn with cuts. A dark liquid seeped out between my scales. My blood looked like black string. My gaze drifted to the dark figure who had thrown the guy off of me.

Ashmay had her fists raised, daring them to fight her.

"Are you okay?" Her voice broke the silence.

"Yes," I murmured.

"Hey, you!" Ashmay turned away from me and back to the bullies who were inching off. "You won't be getting away that easily. Know there will be repercussions for your acts. Harris, don't think I won't tell your dad about this…and Mirah. I'm sure the council would love to hear of this predicament."

"You really think my dad would reprimand me? He would applaud me!" The young merman who had held me down cackled.

"You really think the rulers of Oceanus wouldn't care, Harris?" Ashmay retorted.

With that, they scurried off, but not before Harris turned back to look at Ashmay with a glint in his eyes.

"Now let's get you cleaned up. What do you say?" Ashmay asked. "I know a safe place."

"Anything to get me out of here." I swam up beside her and noticed Ashmay's sorrowful smile. My heart sank slightly as I recognized her pity.

"Follow me. We'll get you something to drink and eat and get you cleaned up a little before you head back to the castle. Don't want Gavin to get upset at the state of you."

"I think you mean Veron. Veron is definitely the one who would flip out if I came back a mess," I corrected.

"Whatever you say. Come on. Follow me. Don't worry, I'll keep you out of abandoned, dead-end alleys." She gave me a wink and swam up out of the gray sandy street.

Ashmay led me over a coral garden, and knocked on the front door of a sand home.

The door was decorated with kelp pressed into designs of merpeople swimming in circles around whales, sharks, and dolphins. They grooved into swirls of yin and yang, showing the way they all lived together. One unified world of water where the air breathers joined those with gills.

"Does everyone feel this way?" I frowned.

"Feel what way?" Ashmay knocked again.

"Feel resentment toward me, like the mermen in the alley. Do most of the people here in Oceanus feel that way?" I asked.

Before Ashmay could respond, the door opened.

"Aye, what are ye two doing here?" Kind eyes greeted us.

"Edmound!" I exclaimed. My chest welled with happiness at the sight of the first kind merperson I had encountered. Yes, Gavin and Veron had saved my life, but I hadn't known Veron yet, and I wouldn't describe Gavin's rescue as warm.

"Well now, don' wait outside, come in, lasses," Edmound moved to the side and allowed us to pass the threshold.

His home was filled with sponge couches, coral chairs, rock

tables, and shell and pearl decorations squeezed between the grains of sand in the wall.

Edmound signaled toward a purple sponge chair in the corner for me to sit. "What're ye two doin' out in this part of town?"

I followed his lead and sat in a room that seemed to be a mixture of a living room and dining room. There was a larger table in the center, but the chairs were more relaxing than the stiff wooden chairs I was used to in a formal dining atmosphere.

"Billie had a run in with Harris and his crew," Ashmay explained. "She has some cuts that I wanted to patch up. Do you have a first aid kit?"

"Yeah, in the loo." Edmound rose.

"No, it's okay, I'll get it," Ashmay swam toward the bioluminescent, blue-lit hallway.

"I wasn' tryin' to eavesdrop, but sound travels in the water." Edmound's gaze dropped to his lap, took a breath, and met my eyes. "Not everyone feels resentment that you're here, lass. I'd say people are mostly curious about ye considerin' a human turned mer hasn' happened in quite a while. At least not here in Oceanus."

"A human changing has happened before?" My eyebrows rose.

"I mean, you know there's talk of it havin' happened. I, personally, have never witnessed it until ye." He shrugged.

A little seahorse, an otter, and several sunfish dolls littered the floor.

"Do you have kids?" I queried.

"Yes, I have a family. A beautiful wife named Penelope and two lovely wee ones. Gregor is six and Melina is eight," he smiled. "They'll actually be home soon. You can meet them."

"I don't know if that's such a good idea." I hesitated. I wasn't sure I was up for more criticism from the people of Oceanus. I'd had enough judgmental eyes follow me through the castle, and the streets weren't safe either. I shivered at the memory of being cornered by the mermen. That could have ended badly if Ashmay hadn't shown up when she did.

Edmound reached over the space separating us and placed his oversized hand on my arm. "Don't be scared, Billie. In fact, my wife has been buggin' me to invite ye over for dinner. She was worried ye were alone and thought ye could use a home-cooked meal."

"In that case, I'd love to stay." I smiled, nerves settling a little. "I am rather tired of staring at the same blank walls day in and day out. But are you sure it's not too last minute?"

"How 'bout you stop worryin' and just enjoy yerself for once? Ye haven't seemed to have much fun for someone who says they love the ocean. Ye sure seem to be loathin' where ye are."

Whoops, was I that obvious?

I cherished people who accepted me with open arms, such as Edmound and Veron, and I loved being able to see a whole new side to the ocean that I hadn't known existed. But I knew I was causing problems. I knew not everyone agreed with allowing a human being to live here. Gavin made sure I knew that.

There was nothing I could do about my position, but it didn't mean I couldn't try enjoying myself more. In fact, maybe instead of staying stuck inside of the castle, away from the rest of Oceanus, I should start lending a hand and proving I wasn't one of the bad guys.

"Did I hear something about dinner?" Ashmay sashayed back into the room. She immediately swam over to me, knelt down, and placed my fin across hers. Ashmay wrapped a long three-inch-wide piece of fabric made of soft coral and sea fan around the bottom of my tail.

I winced.

"Sorry! I added some kelp and sea salt extract to help with any infection. You should feel better in a few days." Ashmay tied the fabric into a knot and patted my tail.

"Can I get ye anythin'? Maybe somethin' to drink or eat?" Edmound offered.

Ashmay perked, "I'll take a—"

"You can get me involved," I interjected.

"Huh?" Edmound raised one thick eyebrow.

"I mean, I want to lend a hand. If I'm stuck here, I might as well be useful or be a part of this place. I know everyone in Oceanus contributes with different duties, so give me a duty." I stared directly into Edmound's eyes. I would not take no for an answer.

"Well, I mean, I don't know. I'm not really the one—"

"What do you do? I know that you help Gavin, but beside that, what do you do?" I interrupted him.

"I go fetch the water from the deep, maybe three or four times per month." Edmound shifted in his seat.

"Take me with you."

"I don't know if that's such a good idea. Ye've only been here for a few weeks and are still gettin' yer bearin's as a mermaid. Maybe ye can talk to the kelp knitters."

"Ahh, come on, Edmound! Look at her," Ashmay pleaded, giving me a wink.

"Ashmay goes down there! I'm sure I'm within the age limitation, if there is one," I continued.

"I don't know. Ashmay is a mermaid," Edmound knotted his hands together.

"I'm a mermaid now too. I can either learn how to be a mermaid or keep being a target for people." I glanced at my wrapped tail and felt the nerves coiled within it.

"And she's strong, right? She must be to survive a human to mermaid transition like that!" Ashmay added.

My ears pricked at the word surviving, but I bit my lip and decided to put a pin in it. "I can do it. I can go collect water with you, with both of you. How hard can it be? It's just opening some water bottles."

"There's a bit more danger to it than that," Edmound retorted.

"Then teach me how to avoid the danger. I will be okay. I want to do something, to prove my worth somehow. And please, don't ask me to knit again."

"I say, let her do it," a female voice chimed in from somewhere near the front door.

Two flashes landed with a thump against Edmound.

High squeals erupted as Edmound let out a reverberating laugh. He threw a curly, long-haired girl up over his head and watched as a wild-haired boy slid down his tail.

The woman had deep hazel eyes, and dark, tightly curled hair that was cut short. Her tail displayed different shades of green in a lime and forest tie-dyed pattern. She placed a platter of fish, seaweed, shellfish, pickled anemone, and sea sponge jerky down on the coffee table.

"Dinner is served! I'm glad you finally made it to our humble abode. I'm Penelope." She smiled and stuck out a hand at me.

I stilled, shocked by her gesture, before firmly grasping her hand. "It's great to meet you. Thank you for the invite."

"Anytime, dear. It's good to get out. It can get awfully dull when you're stuck in the same place."

"She used to live and work in the palace. She was a seaweed weaver," Edmound chuckled.

"Oh. Well, it is nice to get away," I stammered. I picked up a crab leg and cracked it open. Underwater, the white meat easily pulled out of the crevice. It was the perfect mixture of savory and sweet. I followed the bite with pickled anemone. It tasted like pickled cabbage that you would get as a Japanese appetizer, but had the texture of boba.

"You're pretty." Melina sat wide-eyed on the table next to her father. Her eyes were a dark brown that matched her tail. Although, a brown tail at this depth meant it could be any array of colors.

"Why thank you, you're quite beautiful yourself." I smiled as the little girl turned away in a fit of giggles.

"How're you liking it down here?" Penelope inquired before delicately placing a piece of white fish rolled in seaweed into her mouth.

"It's been wonderful from what I've seen. But I think everyone's a little scared to let me out."

Penelope raised an eyebrow at Edmound.

"Why do ye say that?" Edmound asked as he turned his attention away from his wife and toward me, needing only a moment for their unspoken communication.

"I think they are worried about me running back home and ruining everything you have here. Personally, I think it's absurd, because I couldn't find my way home by this point even if I wanted to." I watched as Melina shoved her greens into her napkin.

Ashmay snickered as she plopped down beside me with a handful of food.

"I think you'd be surprised," Penelope muttered.

"Surprised by what?" I pressed.

"Yer part of the ocean now," Edmound answered. "Yer navigation skills of the underwater world are much sharper than they were before. If ye really concentrated on yer skills, ye'd be able to hone in on the sound, salinity, depth, light, and many other factors that could easily lead ye back to shore." His eyes grew big, and a dumbfounded look crossed his face. "I…uh…wasn't…"

"Ya big oaf!" Ashmay rolled her eyes, "I doubt Billie would reveal us to the human world, and she would have figured those things out for herself eventually."

Penelope rubbed her husband's back in solidarity.

I stared at my blue and black painted tail. I had special abilities in the water now. I could find my way home. Maybe I wasn't as imprisoned as I had originally thought.

"Finding my way home won't change my condition anyway. There would be no point," I huffed.

Ashmay reached over and squeezed my hand.

I raised my head.

Hooded eyes the color of the night sky shone back at me. The lights twinkled in her deep eyes, showing support.

"It'll be okay, I promise," Ashmay whispered.

"I'm sorry, we didn't mean to offend you," Penelope said. "I think we're just surprised you're not kicking and screaming to go back home. You must have family, friends, school, and many other things there waiting for you. You had a life there." She reached out across the sandstone coffee table and squeezed my other hand.

Penelope's hands were soft and small. It reminded me of my mother's calming, gentle gestures. A mother's touch.

My chest tightened. "I don't have much to go back to actually, aside from my aunt. I had a life there; I don't have one anymore."

An awkward silence permeated the water.

I stared at the ground, not wanting to see anyone's downturned faces or sorrowful eyes.

I focused on the woven kelp carpet. The kelp was dyed with varying shades of blue, green, violet, and black. A collage of sea turtles, whales, dolphins, sharks, and fish blended together flawlessly to form a circle around a silhouette of a mermaid. Her hair twirled around her body, floating down to her hips, tendrils floating to meet the fins of the animals around her. Interconnected.

"Well, ye have a life here as long as ye want one," Edmound finally filled the silence.

"Yeah, maybe you needed a new face around here in Oceanus," I joked. "Gotta keep things interesting. I just hope I've missed any hazing rituals that occur when your weird folklore actually happens."

"Ye do have to do some bull shark wranglin'." His chuckles turned into full blown guffaws as my face turned paler than the sandy walls.

"Don't forget about eating octopus brains to make her smarter!" Ashmay included.

I gaped. "What?"

"Knock it off! You're scaring the poor girl," Penelope scolded them.

"Yer right, she'll have worse things to worry about if she decides to get water with us from the deep tomorrow." He winked at me, which turned into a wince as Penelope smacked him over the head.

"Serves you right," Ashmay sniggered.

"What? Ye joined in!" Edmound tattled.

"Clearly mine was a joke. Octopuses are clearly too smart for anyone to ever think about eating them. It's just inhumane. It'd be like eating a dolphin!" Ashmay rebutted.

"Melina! Stop feeding Doc your snapper! No dessert if you don't finish your supper," Penelope abruptly yelped.

I peered under the table to see who Doc was, then flew from the chair. My back hit the wall behind me, knocking off painted shells that shattered when they hit the floor.

A four-foot shark swam out one foot from where I had been sitting.

A swirl of black cascaded upward into my face.

A broken shell had cut my hand. I clamped my fingers over the incision, trying to stop more blood from escaping.

I was bleeding in front of a shark! And I wasn't some tasteless human anymore. I was part fish!

Frozen in place, a scream lodged in my throat, Edmound and his family did nothing but stare.

Why weren't they doing anything? This shark was about to have me for dinner!

The dark gray shark moseyed up to me, his caudal fin slowly swishing, until his nose was inches from my tail.

I closed my eyes, ready to feel his teeth sink into me.

Sandpaper rubbed against my scales.

I opened my left eye first, then my right, and found the shark rubbing his side gently against me. Without thinking, I reached my non-bleeding hand down to pet the top of his head.

His tail started wagging furiously back and forth, slapping against the wall. A small grumble escaped his uneven picket-fenced mouth.

"He likes you," Melina assured. "But he likes everyone, except he likes me the best."

"Not-uh! He likes me the best," the youngest whined.

"Hush, you two. And Doc, go to your kennel! You know you're not supposed to be in here when we are eating." At the sound of Penelope's stern voice, the kids quieted, and Doc's fin drooped.

"You have a shark as a pet?" I gasped.

"Duh! Sharks are the best pets! My friend Shelley only has a stingray as a pet. But that's no fun because they can almost never find him unless they accidentally land on him," Melina replied.

Gaping at Melina in disbelief, I noticed the dark waters outside the window behind her. "Does anybody know what time it is?"

"We don't really have time down here, but I'd say it's close to bedtime." Edmound's explanation seemed directed at his children rather than to me.

"Shoot! I need to get back!" I hadn't realized so much time had passed, "I hope no one is looking for me." Yet again I had pulled a disappearing act on Veron, probably worrying the girl sick.

"Do ye want me to take you back?" Edmound floated from his seat.

"No, it's okay. It's the big bright thing that towers over everything else. I don't think it'll be hard to find. Thank you so much, Penelope. Dinner was delicious."

"Of course, dear. You are welcome back anytime."

"Next time, I promise I'll help you clean up too." I hated being a bad house guest.

"P'shaw, unnecessary. I'll see you around," Penelope assured me. She got up from her seat, swam over, and gave me a soft hug.

I returned it, closing my eyes. Next thing I knew, I was being swept up into a bear hug from Edmound.

"I'll pick ye up from the palace tomorrow mornin' after breakfast. If ye have any empty bottles, bring those with ye," Edmound said.

"I'm going to have to head out too. Thank you, as always, for your hospitality. I will see you two tomorrow," Ashmay made finger guns at Edmound, and gave me with a wink. "Are you sure you don't want an escort, Billie?" she asked, looking concerned at my wrapped tail.

"Yes, I'm sure. I'll swim fast and stay out of the streets. Straight to the castle for me," I assured her.

Ashmay gave me a quick hug before leaving.

I waved goodbye to Edmound's children with Doc fast asleep in the other room and left.

SEVENTEEN

"Where have you been?" Gavin hollered as soon as I entered through the main door of the palace. He hit two pieces of metal together, ringing a deafening chime through the building.

"What the heck was that for?" I flinched. "I didn't know becoming hard of hearing would be my punishment." I removed my hands from my ears.

"I need to let the others know I found you. We have people scouring all over for you and I'm not about to go chase after all of them. You can't disappear on us like that."

"I didn't know I had to stay within a specific spot at all times. Maybe you can set up an electric eel that'll shock me when I go out of bounds, really make me feel like the pet I supposedly am."

"Don't be so melodramatic, Billie. You've been gone for hours. Of course, we're going to be worried about you."

"We? You don't need to include yourself in that group just to make either of us feel better," I mockingly laughed.

Gavin shook his head, anger contorting his face. He placed the metal pieces against a wall, preparing to leave.

"And you don't need to run away from the truth either!" I called after him.

"As if you knew the truth," he replied.

My scales felt like they would melt off as the water around me boiled in my anger. How could one person make my body feel like it was on fire? Who did he think he was? I grimaced. I was his assignment, his duty, and nothing more.

He turned to give me one last look before turning down a hall, but stopped when his eyes landed on my wrapped tail. His gaze meandered over my body and I quickly hid my right hand behind my back. Heat rose to my face.

"What...happened?" He was before me in a flash. His hands brushed lightly over the marks on my collar bone before bending down and cautiously reaching out his hand to my tail. His dark eyes looked up, questioning.

"It's okay. Only some scrapes," I said, feeling electricity in my cells.

Gavin unwrapped the seaweed with soft fingers to unveil scrapes and gashes and green and brown flesh in my usually blue tail.

"What happened?" He frowned.

"Uhh…I had a run-in with some merpeople, I think Ashmay called one of them Harris, but she—" I nonchalantly pushed a loose strand of hair behind my ear.

His jaw tightened when he saw the cut on my palm.

I dropped my hand.

"I'm going to kill him," he seethed.

I shrugged. "I should've been more careful or told someone where I was going. I was just so tired of being cooped up here."

His face softened. "I am sorry this happened. I'm not trying to keep you locked up or a prisoner. I just want you to be safe." He put his hand over the cuts and closed his eyes. His skin was soft and smooth, like the ocean naturally exfoliated him. A thrill at his touch ran up my tail, hitting my skin where goosebumps peaked out. His nostrils flared, and the water grew hot, so hot that my tail burned. I bit my lip through the pain, refusing to cry out or break his focus. After a few seconds, he pulled away and I saw burned scabs over my cuts.

"What did you do?" I gasped. There was a slight tingle but no more pain.

"Have you noticed that when you feel a strong emotion the water changes around you?" Gavin rewrapped my wounds.

"Yeah."

"Water gets rid of body heat twenty times faster than air, and with our connection to our surroundings, it is somehow tied to our emotions as well. Anger, distress, pain, fear, happiness…and…" he trailed off, staring into my eyes.

Butterflyfish erupted in my stomach.

His fingers ran along my tail, sending a chill up my spine. "And other strong feelings," he hummed.

I gulped, ignoring the nerves writhing in my stomach.

"Get the water hot enough, you can use it to cauterize wounds."

"Billie! You're okay!" A scream of delight broke our reverie.

Gavin dropped my tail and retreated a couple of feet.

"Yeah, um, sorry Veron." I tore my eyes away from Gavin as he focused on the wall with his stern face back in place. "I decided to go out on the town and ended up having dinner with Edmound and his family." I returned Veron's suffocating embrace, feeling the tension in my body ease.

"It's okay. I know it's boring being stuck inside. I'm glad you got out and saw Oceanus a little. What'd you think?" Veron pulled away with excitement in her eyes.

I couldn't bring myself to tell her about the creeps. "It was great. The market was so busy, and it was nice to feel like I was a regular merperson. And I met Edmound's pet shark, which nearly gave me a heart attack." I held my hands over my heart, tilted my head back, and pretended to faint.

Veron broke into giggles, and I joined in myself.

"Yeah, they have a nurse shark. He's super sweet. It's the ones who try to keep tiger sharks as pets that you have to look out for."

"People try to keep tiger sharks? Here?" I gulped.

Veron laughed again. "Yeah, but you don't have to worry about them. Usually, it's the merpeople on the outskirts of town."

"Good thing I didn't try to go there. I may not have come back at all," I joked.

"Or just missing an arm," Veron nudged me in the side.

"As long as it's my left arm. I use my right one too much."

We laughed.

"I'm exhausted. I feel like I swam a marathon. I'm sorry I worried you. I'll try not to do it again," I promised.

"I'm just glad you're okay."

"By the way," I paused. I didn't want Veron to fret over anything else, but the others would be expecting me tomorrow. I bit the inside of my cheek.

Veron's forehead crinkled.

"I'm planning to go with Edmound and Ashmay tomorrow to collect water. But I don't have to go if you don't want me to. I don't want to worry you again," I blurted out.

"It's all right. It's a pretty common thing for merpeople to do, and it'd be good for you. But you'd better be careful, missy." Veron stuck out her tongue.

"Really?" My eyes brightened before a pout crossed my face. "I should get permission."

"Don't worry, I'll take care of my brother. You'll need water bottles too. I'll collect some for you."

"Great, thanks! I'll get them from you in the morning. I'm pretty beat. After having to fight for my life against a nurse shark." I smiled, knowing nurse sharks were nothing to be afraid of.

Veron gave me another hug. "All right. I'll see you in the morning. Sweet dreams."

"Night." I waved at Veron as she swam off.

Thank goodness Veron hadn't noticed my wrapped tail or asked why I had run into Edmound and Ashmay. I didn't want to hide it from her, but I was fine. I didn't need to cause her unnecessary worry.

I turned back to Gavin, but he was gone.

EIGHTEEN

My eyes drooped lazily, the shadows cast by the bioluminescence moving around like an ant colony, lulling me back to sleep.

Veron had woken me up after only a few hours of sleep to inform me Edmound was downstairs.

I had brushed my teeth after eating a light meal of sea scallops and sea grapes. Had I known we would have had such an early start, I wouldn't have agreed to go the very next day. However, I had, and I would abide by my commitments. I was trying to win points and considering this was the first time I would actually be doing something useful in Oceanus, I wasn't about to back out.

Edmound and I swam to an arena on the outskirts of town, where merpeople were bustling about with their morning duties. He left me to go check in, but with nothing to do, I drifted back to sleep on a rock in the corner.

A shadow fell over me. It was noticeable even with my eyes closed.

"We should get ye ready before ye fall asleep and I have to carry ye with us."

"Sorry, Edmound. Yesterday was just a long day, and I didn't know I would be waking up so early. Not that it's a problem," I added. I didn't want him to think I was placing blame on him. I pried open my eyes and peered up at the mountainous merman.

He smiled, wrapping his thick carrot-like fingers around my hand and pulling me from the ground.

Time to join the herds.

"Come on, lass. Let's get you situated." He swam toward a kelp tent where a group of people submerged their hands in buckets of red liquid to lather their torsos and tails.

We pushed our way to the front of the line through the troves of merpeople. Despite Edmound's warnings that this was dangerous, the group of people was large and filled with determined faces.

At one point, I glimpsed Ashmay. Her usually bright face was sullen with seriousness. I hadn't had the chance to shout hello before she was off again to continue doing whatever duties everyone but me knew about.

The tent was stuffy. I hadn't noticed when I was hidden in the corner away from the crowds, but the water was rather hot. Due to the constant hustle, the water had heated up, and if I was on land, I had no doubt I'd be sweating.

I smelled my armpits like I would have at home, but got only a whiff of the earthy sea salt.

"You need to cover your body in the powdered red sponge. It'll help hide you from deep predators." Black eyes stared at me from the opposite side of the bucket.

"As welcoming as ever," I replied.

Gavin handed me a small bowl filled with red matte liquid.

I snagged it and weeded my way through the mass of people. Fins swiped me in the face a few times since people were swimming through all levels of the water column. Unlike land, where everyone walked on the same level, everyone here swam wherever their tails could fit.

Back in my cozy corner, where I didn't have to worry about

dodging fins, bottles, spears, or hands, I inspected the sludge.

The liquid was red with shimmers of orange. The colors were beautiful, but I had no clue how to apply it. I scooped some into my hand, and watched as it slowly started to disperse into the water like food dye.

"That won't do. Now, will it?" A light laugh echoed above me.

The rest of the red dispersed into the water. A friendly smile glimmered down at me. I didn't recognize him, but his laugh had a charm to it. It was contagious and welcoming.

He drifted down to my level.

Face to face, I was caught by the glint in his soft brown eyes, showing off dots of amber. His black hair was cut short to keep it from flowing into his face.

"Do you need some help?" he offered.

"If you don't mind," I said with a smile of my own.

"It would be my absolute pleasure." He placed his hand on my shoulder to steady me while he scooped out a handful of the muck. He lathered it over my shoulders and back like he was putting on sunscreen. Again, he laughed. Not at me in particular, and I couldn't help but join in. This merman was the epitome of a morning person, and I was here for it.

Slowly, I became what only could be described as a sparkly tomato.

Our laughter was almost inaudible in the room with everyone talking among themselves, but it still seemed to liven up the place.

"Do I really have to wear this?" I asked.

"Of course you do. Unless you want to be eaten by the deep sea monster, whose teeth are as piercing as an ice pick and who has a specific taste for mer flesh." He dropped a glob on top of my hair, and using my fingers, I brushed it through the strands.

My stomach dropped. I didn't know there was a creature that specifically hunted merpeople.

He laughed at my saucer-wide eyes. "I'm just messing with you.

There are animals we don't want to be seen by, and wearing this red makes us invisible to them since the red-light spectrum doesn't pierce that deeply into the water."

"No sea monster?"

"None of the ones I talked about. It's too easy to get newbies with that one," he smiled again.

Did this man ever frown?

"Oy! Spaansa! We need your help with the bottles," a merman hollered from the opposite wall.

"Duty calls." He gave me a quick rub on the arm for encouragement.

"No worries, I can figure it out from here. By the way, I'm Billie."

"I know who you are, but I see you don't know who I am," he said.

"You're Spaansa," I replied with a smirk.

"You got it! See you out on the field, kid," He turned and swam to the other side of the area, but not before giving me one last friendly smile.

Over the next hour, I managed to cover my body from head to tail in the shimmery red paste. Once it was on my skin, it didn't drift into the water, the adhesion of my skin and scales held it in place.

I also acquired a netted bag filled with about twenty empty water bottles. They were compressed to take up as little room as possible, making them easier to carry. The netted bag had two straps to wear like a backpack.

Around me, most merpeople had only covered portions of their bodies by adding stripes intermittently.

I had covered myself entirely. My face flushed red, not that anyone could tell, and I instantly felt like a fool.

A giggle came from behind me. "Oh my gosh, Billie, you only needed to break up your silhouette to hide from predators, not become fully invisible."

I grimaced at Ashmay, embarrassed that I hadn't looked around before covering my body in the red paint.

"It's okay. Hold still." Ashmay grabbed a rag off a table and with a flurry she circled around me.

My body turned into a swirl of my natural colors, starting across my eyes and ending around my caudal fin.

"Thanks," I muttered.

"Don't even worry about it. You didn't know. It's a totally understandable mistake. It's all fine now, and I think I'm the only one who noticed. Thankfully, with my red tail and hair, my silhouette is already broken up, so predators don't see me as a meal, but just random pieces." Ashmay winked.

The corners of my mouth turned up.

Everyone bustled from the arena and headed into the open morning water.

The water was fresh and cool against my face. I inhaled deeply, relishing the lightness as the crowds thinned. Some merpeople carried other bags filled with something other than bottles, but I couldn't tell what was inside of them.

Spaansa swam to the front of the crowd.

"Good morning, everyone! Thank you for coming out for this trip. You know I always welcome everyone who's here to help." He smiled, of course.

The crowd of people in the back slowly rose. Since I was a few rows back, I only rose a few inches. The entire crowd moved until we had positioned ourselves into stadium-style seating so that everyone could easily see Spaansa. Our attention was solely on him.

I guess he was more important than I realized.

"I'm sure most of you know who I am and what I do, but for those of you who don't, I'm the navigating officer." His eyes flashed to me.

I bowed my head in gratitude. He was trying his best to help me, knowing I had very little idea of what I was about to endure.

Everyone else was a pro.

He continued, "I will guide you all through the realms of the deep. Your eyes will adjust, and you'll be able to see just fine down there. You may see creatures you have never come across, but keep a wary distance. As long as you follow the path I set out for you, we should have no problems. The journey shouldn't take more than five days."

Five days? I had no idea that this would take so long. I didn't have any blankets or food. Edmound, Ashmay, Veron, and Gavin hadn't said anything to me about the time frame. I just thought I'd be gone for the day. How far away could the deep water possibly be? We were already pretty deep.

"Swim swift and light, and tread water. Let's head out!" Spaansa spun around and took off.

I didn't even need to start swimming because the rush of people shoved me forward. I swiped my tail, trying not to hit anyone, but my heart rate sped up, already overwhelmed.

Some merpeople stopped moving, taking a short break to chat with someone, but they still moved with the group because of the current we created together.

Spaansa worked his tail hard, leading the group. He reminded me of the lead goose breaking through the wind to provide an easier path for those who followed. Unlike the V-formation of geese, we were an amoeba-shaped blob, and no one traded positions with Spaansa to take on the brunt of the work.

The terrain changed the deeper we swam. Ground that was once littered with the spiking shells of conchs, where outcrops of rocks hid lobsters in their nooks, and mini sandstorms stirred up from hidden sting rays became nothing more than a barren landscape. The sand was no longer molded into homes for the merpeople, but had become a puddy that was as easy to disturb as the muddy banks on the side of a pond. We saw fewer animals, only the occasional sleeping shark nestled in the caverns or a rare school of fish that moved in perfect unison as though their numbers shared one mind. The blue lanterns grew brighter, reminding me it was getting darker with every movement downward we took.

My fin muscles became sore and soon I was dragging myself along, praying a break would come soon. I wasn't as strong a swimmer as everyone else. Yes, I spent a lot of time in the ocean, but as a human without a tail.

The water no longer streamlined past my body. It whipped across my face, sending chills through my body. The temperature turned frigid, causing icy pain in my chest with each breath.

I paused

"You okay?"

My eyes fluttered open. "Yeah, I'm fine. Go ahead, I'll catch up."

I hadn't realized that Gavin had also made his way to the back of the group. What was he doing back here? He's definitely a 'front of the pack' kind of guy. Ready for action. Yet, here he was. Speaking of him being here, did he usually collect water? Neither Veron nor Edmound had mentioned it as a usual duty of his, and as busy as he always seemed, I was surprised to see him at all.

Oh. He was babysitting me.

"If you continue to wait any longer, I'm afraid you won't be able to find the group in order to catch up." Gavin looked me up and down. He chuckled when my disheveled hair slapped across my red face. Colored from exhaustion, not ink.

"Sorry I'm a normal person who is trying something new for the first time and not having an easy go at it. How about you run a marathon on land with no previous training, and then we'll talk," I snapped.

His lips thinned. "I'm just looking out for you."

"I don't need you to look out for the poor human girl. Don't you have some more important business to take care of?" I glared at him.

He threw his hands out in exasperation. "I'm trying to help you in your new setting!"

I scoffed. "I know it may come as a shock to you, but I've actually been in the ocean before and miraculously survived without you beside me."

"All I'm saying is we know a lot more about your world than you do about ours. We've taken a lot of time to study the human race. We need to understand you to avoid you," he explained while taking measured breaths.

"Why do you need to avoid us? You act like all humans are these terrible creatures. You know, it's really offensive the way you speak of humans considering, well, I'm human!" I retorted.

"I know. I'm sorry. We just know humans are very obsessed with advancement and discoveries. Merpeople feel no need to become yet another thing to be discovered, figured out, or mapped on some biological chart. We'd just rather keep to ourselves."

"I get that. You're worried about what we're doing to the oceans, but don't you think if you somehow worked with human society to let them know, a difference could be made?" If only Gavin could see the good in people instead of thinking we were something to shy away from.

"Maybe one day, Billie. In a perfect world, that would be great. For now, let's worry about you or you'll never be able to do this for days." He placed both hands on my shoulders. He was strong, warm, and under the weight of his hands, I stopped shivering.

"I look like a candy cane." I glowered up at him.

Gavin gave a puzzled look.

Right, merman. He probably didn't know what a candy cane was.

"Imagine lionfish coloring on a stick," I murmured.

Gavin threw his head back and barked out laughter.

I stared wide-eyed at the foreign gesture. The heartiness of his amusement swelled within me. It was impossible to hold my scowl any longer and I broke into a fit of giggles.

Out of the corner of my eye, I glimpsed a plum-colored tail. I jumped, realizing it was close enough for me to notice the movement and see the color. Which meant it was way too close for comfort.

"Did you see that?" I pointed into the dark waters to the right.

"What?" He searched the waters wiping at his eyes, and his smile faded.

"I thought I saw…there!" I pointed behind him to a myriad of blue and purple hair. There had been a silvery glint in the water, like a knife.

Gavin turned, but it was gone. "It's probably another merperson from our group." His eyes darted as he searched the dark. "We better get going," he quickly added as he grabbed my hand to swim away, positioning himself between me and what he claimed was merely another merperson. He was clearly not telling me something.

"Gavin…" I looked toward the group, or rather what should have been the group. Instead, there was only darkness.

"Shoot. We waited too long. We got left behind. When Spaansa sets off, it's nearly impossible to get him to stop or slow down." His brows pulled together in thought.

"We got left behind?" I squeaked. "Should we turn back?"

"Don't worry, I've done this plenty of times. We're not too far behind, and I know the first campsite really well. I used to take emergency trips there myself for water. We'll just have to swim quickly."

"Not a problem." Yeah, I was sore, but I'd pull through, especially if it got me out of the creepy, dark ocean.

Gavin nodded. "All right, let's go." Pulling my hand, he tugged me forward. "Stay close."

156

KRISTEN BRADDOCK

NINETEEN

After hours of swimming, Gavin paused.

I took the time to catch my breath and took a swig of some water Gavin had the foresight to bring. The ocean continued to get colder. Needle-like sensations pricked against my skin, but the scales protected my tail from feeling them.

"Time for a break?" I paused beside him.

His teeth clenched and eyebrows drew together. "Something isn't right." He held out his lantern, trying to cover a space larger than the ten-foot diameter around us. It only showed more sand with a couple of fingernail sized crabs burying themselves back into their burrows.

I said nothing.

Gavin mumbled to himself, "There was a current coming from the north. It was stronger than I predicted, and it must have pushed us south of where we should be. I don't know this area as well, we need to head north but heading into the current will take us a long time to get to where we need to be. We are easily five miles south...or southeast...or southwest."

"South or southeast or southwest? Are you kidding me? We're lost? We're in the middle of the deep ocean with barely any supplies, and we're lost?" I paled.

"It's going to be fine," he said in a monotone voice, which gave me no confidence.

"Fine? I'm covered in red goo so some creatures that have the longest tooth to body ratio in the world don't see and attack me, and you say we're fine! We have no weapons, we have no map, we have no concept of where we are! Fine? Ha. We've been moving for six hours and we still have five miles to go, against a current no less. This is not fine!" I fumed. My knuckles turned white. "Are we going to die?"

Gavin turned, catching me by my shoulders. "We are not going to die. We are perfectly fine. I promise. I'm not going to let anything happen to you, and we're going to rejoin the group."

Lost within the depths of his eyes, my mouth hung open. His hands were so warm a shiver ran through me. His gaze dropped to my lips, and mine dropped to his. My breathing slowed until it matched his. A part of me hoped he would kiss me, and that terrified me. I couldn't want him. We came from different worlds. I didn't understand his, the same way he didn't understand mine. And yet, every nerve ending in my body electrified when I was near him.

His eyes softened, and his grip lightened until his hands fell away, breaking whatever moment we had. "I do think we've completely exhausted ourselves and we need a rest before we head north. They have enough lanterns that once we're within a mile, we'll be able to see their glow. It'll help direct us toward them. Let's find a safe spot to rest and we'll start back up in a few hours. We. Are. Fine," he reassured me.

"Okay." My muscles relaxed. It was funny, I trusted him and knew with every particle in my body I was safe with him.

Gavin found a hill of sand about four feet high, just enough to protect us from the current caused by upwelling from deeper areas of the ocean.

From what I learned, it was the kind of nutrient rich water we wanted to collect, but it also meant the water was freezing.

We stuck our lanterns into the sand, and placed our packs on the ground to use them as pillows. Lying down perpendicular to the hill, our entire bodies hid from the biting current. Our shoulders were centimeters away from each other as we lay on our backs.

"Hey, Gavin?" I murmured.

"Yeah?" His warmth emanated through the water.

"What's your favorite part of being a merman?"

He was silent.

Two minutes passed. I counted.

"Sorry, it wasn't my place to ask." I interlocked my fingers over my churning stomach.

"No, it's not that. No one's ever asked me that before. I had to think about it. It would be like asking 'What's your favorite part of being human?' It's not something you ever wonder because...you just are." He thought for a few moments more before whispering, "The endlessness."

"The endlessness?" I pursed my lips at the answer. I would have said all the fish, dolphins, and reefs. Or the fact a person could have a pet shark as a dog.

"Yeah. It's as though everything can just keep going. I can swim in any direction— up, down, sideways. I can do flips or enter my room from a window. Gravity seems like such a drag on land. Even though we live down here, I have endless places to explore, endless new species to see. It all feels so personal, as though my limits are so far away. It's...endless."

"Wow," I breathed. I had never thought of it that way, and I couldn't help but agree.

He sounded so peaceful when he spoke. I looked over at his face and his usual rigid set was nowhere to be seen. It was tender with a far-off gaze.

His jaw was still sharp, but with an artist's sculpt to it. His lower lip stuck out farther than his top lip. His eyebrows arched like mountains over his crisp dark eyes sparkling with the flickering bioluminescent lights. His hair rippled with the slight movements of the water, spreading the strands apart to give it volume, smooth enough to run fingers through.

I blinked. I couldn't be distracted by some boy, and this was Gavin! The person who constantly infuriated me, who made my blood bubble, who could be so hard-headed I felt even if I took a sledgehammer to that head, it wouldn't crack.

"What's your favorite part of being a mermaid?" He turned to me with a lopsided smile.

My fingers intertwined tighter. "I don't know. For me, it's all so magical. I've always loved the ocean, so getting to see it like this has been unbelievable. I guess this is the first time in years that I've felt happy. Being here, being a mermaid, has brought me a sense of adventure and happiness I haven't felt in a long time."

"Why's that?"

I turned my head away to hide the tears brimming in my eyes. I wasn't going to cry about this, not now, not in front of Gavin. A bulge formed in my throat. It hurt. I tried to swallow it, but gulping down losing both parents and everything that entailed was no easy feat.

"Shhh."

Did he seriously just tell me to be quiet?

He reached into his sack and pulled out a blanket-sized piece of fabric.

How much did he put in that satchel? It was like Mary Poppins's bag!

He tossed the fabric around the lanterns.

Everything went pitch black.

"What're you doing?" I whispered.

I sat up and hugged my tail close to my body.

Gavin's measured breaths came from my right, his heat permeating the water.

Then there was a sound in the distance.

It traveled to me like a train's horn. The sounds were long, going from high, like a caw of a falcon, to low like the rumble of a diesel engine.

"Do you hear them?" He breathed.

"Yes," I whispered.

The vocal symphony of whales cascaded around us.

Without the lights, my hearing came to life. Four whales hummed together like they were the crickets of the ocean.

"The mom is calling to her baby. It seems the baby got distracted by something and started to stray off," Gavin explained the tunes.

"What kind of whales are they?" My eyes widened. Even after listening to music my entire life, I had never heard anything so heavenly.

"They're humpback whales. It's not very common to hear their song. They're south of us, so I bet no one at camp or back in Oceanus is hearing this right now. We could be the only ones listening. Now, the mother is cooing to her baby, telling the baby how much she loves him."

"How do you know what they're saying? Can you speak whale?" I was talking so quietly I wasn't sure if he heard me.

He gave a small chuckle. His sound blended perfectly in tune with the whales' song—a duet. "No, I don't speak whale. There are no specific words or anything. You can just understand the gist of what is happening. My father used to take me as a young boy to go listen to the whales. Every year, when the gray whales' migratory path passed Oceanus, he would take me out. We would sit in total darkness, and he would explain to me what was happening with the whales. Eventually, I started to pick it up myself. Humpback whales are similar. It's like they have a different dialect. But I've never actually heard them before."

We lay back down and listened as the whales called to one

another.

What would it be like if life was a constant musical and we sung our words to one another? If it sounded anything like the whales, it'd be fantastic.

The song of the whales never grew faint, and it lulled me to sleep.

I dreamed of whales.

I awoke shivering. Goosebumps littered my body and when my tail moved, the scales felt stiff. I lay there for a few moments, listening to Gavin's deep breath.

I didn't want to wake him, but my body ached from the stiffness. I should swim around a bit, and get my blood flow going to warm myself up.

Pressing my palms into the sand, I collapsed back onto my back. My muscles ached from hours of swimming, and combined with the cold, my body locked up.

Gavin mumbled in his sleep.

I froze, not wanting to wake him. After a few seconds without another murmur from him, I attempted to get up again—success.

I shuffled in the dark until I found one of the lights. Loosening part of the wrap around the light, I used my body to block the glow.

Making out the basic black shape of Gavin and the sand mound we hid behind, I took the light and swam up the slope. I held the light farther in front of me.

The whales were gone, it was deathly quiet, and the light displayed mere sand.

I swam in small circles, enough to warm up my muscles, but not stray away in the dark by retracing my strokes to know where the ridge was.

Sand, sand, rock, sand, rock, sand, crab, sand, sand, sand. Not a whole lot out here.

At first, I ignored movement to my left, thinking it was a wave of my red tail. After my momentary brain lapse, I stopped and turned my head to the left.

Nothing.

I crept farther into the darkness, still holding the light, until I came to a rock wall. It was taller and wider than what the light shone upon.

Again, a flash of red to the left.

I snapped my head. Bounding forward, I came to a corner in the wall, and stopped.

Floating in the corner was a Dumbo octopus, resembling a little kid's blobby drawing. Now that I was closer, the octopus morphed into a beige color, trying to blend into the sand around it. Its legs were much shorter than the typical octopus I had seen before; most of its body was a round little head. It looked like a balloon with large eyes watching me in return.

It shrank away.

"It's okay, little guy. I'm not going to hurt you." I backed off a little, becoming docile and speaking gently.

The octopus inched forward.

I smiled. Reaching my hand forward, it backed up a few inches.

The octopus eyed me suspiciously.

My hand extended out all the way, but I didn't move forward.

After a few heartbeats, the octopus crawled into my hand. It had a rougher texture than expected, but was quite squishy.

It changed colors—pink to beige to yellow to pink again. That's when I noticed its peculiar ears. They flapped up and down, moving in rhythm with my touch.

I snickered at the Dumbo-like appearance.

Abruptly, it turned a deep red, hopped off, and flew back to the crevice of the wall before reverting to its beige color.

Cocking my head, I swiveled as a huge shape lunged toward me.

I skirted to the right. My right shoulder slammed against the wall.

Teeth snapped in my face.

I heard myself scream. Using the light, I smashed the beast in the face.

It swam out of reach of my light, its movements sluggish and slow.

As it swam away, I glanced at its tail. It was a shark, probably about twelve feet long. Could I outrun it? I looked around wildly. I had no idea where Gavin was. With the wall behind me, the only direction to flee was into the darkness where the shark had just gone.

My eyes wide, I searched the darkness but couldn't see anything. I gripped the handle of the light.

The little bioluminescent flecks floated in front of my face. No. They were in front of my face!

I inspected the bulb and saw a crack. My light was escaping.

As the plankton seeped out, the light dimmed.

I gulped down my rising panic. Should I make a run for it? Then I'd be out in the open. At least here, the wall protected my backside.

The light faded further.

I couldn't move even if I wanted to or I'd wind up in darkness. Sharks were ambush predators. Definitely not the situation I wanted to end up in.

Sipping on tiny breaths, my heart pounded. It felt like my tail was stuck in cement. I couldn't move. My hands shook with fear.

Help. Please leave. Please be gone. I could call for Gavin. Or use the remnants of the lamp to protect myself. But once I left the rock, I'd have to protect myself from all sides. It might be best to wait here. Gavin would realize I was gone, or I hoped he would.

A dark shape passed on the edge of darkness. It was waiting for me.

I was frozen in place, too scared to move, too scared to cry for help.

The light cast a three-foot radius from me to the darkness.

The shark lunged.

I jabbed my lamp into the shark's gills.

The shark sputtered. The bottom of the lamp caught in the side of the shark. Its head thrashed from side to side

Holy crap. I almost got mauled by a shark. I had to protect myself…from a shark!

The shark's forehead protruded to form a horn at the tip of its head. It was long and pointy like a javelin to spear its enemies. I couldn't take my eyes off its teeth. Long and sharp as needles, with a jerk the entire jaw extended outward. The unhinged jaw shot out nearly a foot with a snap of its teeth.

It was a thing of nightmares. My breath sputtered in short bursts.

The shark came closer.

My heart rate rocketed. I picked up a rock from the ground and threw it at the beast. The rock hit square in the eye—bullseye.

This angered the shark more. Its attention fully redirected at me. It stopped thrashing.

Oh no. I made things worse.

It watched my every move.

My hands shook at my sides. Breathe. Concentrate. If it attacks, I'll jump to the side. Just keep breathing, I reminded myself.

The remnants of the light escaped and when the bioluminescent flecks nearly went out, all I could see were black eyes glaring at me. Everything seemed to slow down. My heart, my breath, the swish of its tail.

It lunged.

I let out a deafening shriek. Tucking myself into a ball, I fell to the ground with a soft thud.

Fail. My fight or flight seemed to be broken.

But nothing happened.

I uncovered my face. Peeking between my fingers, I saw Gavin holding the end of the light pole still lodged in the gills of the shark, keeping it at bay while the shark snapped at him.

"On the count of three, we're going to swim up. We're going to swim fast and hard. It's not a pursuit predator so it won't chase us," he said through clenched teeth.

"Okay," I gulped.

"I need you to help me push the stick. We need to push the shark away from us or else we won't have enough room," Gavin's strength was waning. "Grab it now and shove on my count."

I grasped the end with clammy fingers. "Got it."

The other lantern was strapped to Gavin's back, leaving both of our hands free.

"One...two...three!"

We shoved as hard as we could and raced upward before seeing if we'd had any effect.

I was right beside Gavin, flapping my fin as hard as I could. We went up and over the ridge and continued to speed away. My lungs were burning when Gavin slowed until we both came to a stop.

"What was that thing?" I huffed, placing my hands on my chest where it burned.

"A goblin shark. Usually, they don't act that way toward something so big. You must've intervened with what it was hunting." Gavin placed his hands on his side while he panted.

"How'd you know where I was?" I wondered.

"I heard you scream. It took me a few moments to find your dimming light."

"Yeah, I broke the lamp."

"I noticed. You really buried it into that shark. I'm surprised it didn't run off."

"I'm surprised I'm alive. Thanks, by the way. You know, for saving me." I gave a faint smile.

"You saved yourself. You would have been toast long before

that if you hadn't fought. It may have even chased you if you had tried to run."

"But you said it wouldn't chase us!"

"They usually don't, and since there were two of us, I didn't think it would, but it was acting so weird that if it were only you, I wouldn't have been surprised."

"Think? You really need to start using words that add a little confidence."

He chuckled before passing over my pack. "We should get going now that we have our blood pumping. The current has died down a lot so it shouldn't take us too long to get there. We'll reach everyone before they set off." Gavin squeezed my shoulder in reassurance.

TWENTY

hether it was the adrenaline, the anticipation of meeting up with everyone, or the enhanced abilities—I was finally getting used to being a mermaid—I kept up with Gavin the entire time. I grinned with triumph when I pointed out the lights in the distance before he'd seen them.

An hour after spotting the lights, we finally joined the group. Everyone was waking up, eating breakfast, and filling the water with conversation.

We collapsed seconds after arriving at the camp.

"I've been looking for you two everywhere! I have breakfast for you!" Ashmay bounced over to us with a liveliness further draining me. But she had plates of food.

My mouth watered, or would have, if I were on land.

"You're heaven sent," Gavin muttered. He grabbed the food and water bottles from Ashmay, quickly tossing one in my direction. It was biscuit-like with fish eggs inside.

My eyes rolled into the back of my head. It was delicious. I hadn't realized how hungry I was until Gavin passed me a second biscuit. I had finished the first in under a minute.

"Woah. You two are eating like you haven't eaten in a day," Ashmay gaped.

We gave each other sidelong glances.

"Oh dear, what happened?" Ashmay cocked her head.

"We may have gotten lost." I gave a one-shouldered shrug.

"Lost?" Ashmay's jaw hung open. "But Gavin, you never get lost. Did you spend the night in the deep sea by yourselves?"

"There was a current," Gavin muttered.

"Yeah, but we are here now! Safe and sound!" I squeezed Ashmay's hand.

"Good thing you didn't come across the Abyssals," Ashmay said.

"The what?" I asked.

"It's a group of merpeople that—" Ashmay was stopped by Gavin's glare.

Wait, the blue and purple hair I saw, could it have been one of them? Was that why he was so freaked out? I knew he had been hiding something earlier! If I could kill with a look, he'd be dead right now.

"I'm going to go check on the rest of the group. I'm glad you two are safe," Ashmay shimmied away before things got too awkward.

"Gavin." I narrowed my eyes at him.

"Don't worry about it. We are fine. Ashmay doesn't know what she's talking about. I'm going to go check in with Spaansa."

Gavin left before I could press, leaving me alone to heat the cold water with my annoyance.

After everything we had been through together, he still didn't trust me.

The next four days were spent going to three different sites to collect water. The different sites each held unique nutrients.

I tirelessly unscrewed water bottles to hand them to Ashmay or Edmound, avoiding Gavin the rest of the trip.

There was a unique trick to getting the water already inside the bottle out. A hollow reed was pushed inside the water bottle. The bottle was held upside down at an angle, and the merperson blew into the straw which pushed the water out of the bottle but did not allow new water to come in until the person turned the bottle upright. The water bottle would then fill with the freezing nutrient rich water, which we would cap and store.

I managed to successfully do this once, and in my bouncing excitement all of the water spilled out. For the angles and breath needed, it took me about fifteen minutes to fill one water bottle.

I didn't like failure. The whole point of me coming was to prove I could help the mer community and prove I could be one of them. It was disheartening, so I decided I'd rather stay in the comfort zone of taking the caps off.

When all the water bottles were filled, we returned to the original campsite before making the final trek back.

The water grew colder as night set in; the temperature drop was the only way to tell time when we were this deep. That night, I curled up into a ball and dreamed of my bed back in Oceanus.

I awoke to a grunt and thud.

A hundred feet from where I slept, a merman had collapsed on the ground.

I jumped up, and swam over to him. I had seen him a few times filling water bottles, and I recognized his deep purple hair.

His eyes were huge, his mouth agape, but no sound came out.

"Sir, are you okay?" I studied his body for signs of trauma. A little wound reddened on the top of his hand below his thumb.

He had probably been pricked by a sea urchin. If only we had vinegar, then I could dissolve the spine within a few hours.

His eyes glazed over. All he did was point toward a pile of rocks.

"What is it?" I wondered.

He pointed, still no sound, not even a breath.

"You need to breathe," I coaxed.

He didn't. He only pointed.

I went over to the rocks and after scouring the area, two holes opened on the side of a head. The little octopus was hard to spot, camouflaged with the rocks.

"The octopus?" I turned back toward the man, but he didn't respond.

I shrugged and reached for the creature.

Dark brown spots appeared all over its body with a miraculous bright blue around them.

Mesmerized by the colors, my hand continued forward despite a warning flashing in the back of my mind. My mouth hung open as there was another flash of blue.

It was gorgeous! I'd never seen an octopus turn these colors before. The hues seemed like they glowed.

"Stop!" Gavin grasped my wrist and yanked me away.

"Ow! What was that for?" I glowered at him, rubbing my wrist from his grip.

"It's venomous." Gavin frowned at me. "It's one of the most poisonous creatures in the ocean. It has enough venom to kill around twenty-seven mermen from a single bite. And it shouldn't be here." The last part was a low murmur I didn't think he intended for me to hear.

The octopus, no bigger than seven inches, continued pulsing its magnificent colors as it crept into a crevice.

My eyes widened. The blue was a warning, and like an idiot, I was drawn to it instead. Gavin had even mentioned color-changing was a warning sign, and I had almost touched the thing right in front of him. I mentally face palmed myself. I didn't want to be seen as a stupid human, but touching anything unfamiliar seemed pretty idiotic.

Gavin's face showed no sign of emotion as he studied me. He glanced at my red wrist, and a grimace flashed across his face.

I let out a steadying breath, and headed back to the hurt merman.

His lips were blue, and his eyes brimmed with silent tears. Even though we were underwater, the differing salt ratios made the shimmering water look different than teardrops.

Others had started tending to him. They were crafting a makeshift carrier out of reeds and seaweed.

"What's wrong with him?" I mumbled to Gavin.

"His respiratory system is shutting down. It happens within a few minutes. He'll die of suffocation." His voice was low.

"What?" I jolted backward. "Why doesn't someone give him the anti-venom?"

"There isn't any."

A group of merpeople carried him back toward Oceanus.

My heart clenched. If Gavin hadn't stopped me, I'd be right there beside him. Dying. Oceanus was hours away. This man was going to die before they reached it, and his family wouldn't get to say goodbye. There would be no final words, no closure. Just like my parents. At least the family would have a body to mourn.

My throat closed.

"Okay, everyone, I know we're all tired, but grab a quick bite to eat, and then let's head home," Spaansa boomed from above our heads.

"Let's go home." Gavin squeezed my hand for a quick second before swimming away.

I nodded. Let's go home.

TWENTY-ONE

Veron burst into my room unannounced to find me curled up in a ball on my bed.

I peeked over my shoulder to see who it was.

"What's up?" A worried crease formed between Veron's eyebrows as she plopped on the bed. "Is everything okay?"

I nodded, avoiding eye contact.

"You can talk to me, you know?" Veron pleaded.

I nodded again, but my chest suddenly tightened, and my eyes brimmed with tears.

"Seriously, what's going on?" Veron threw her arms around me.

I shook my head, the tears blurring my vision at the loving warmth of Veron's embrace. Unable to hold back any longer, I silently cried against Veron's shoulder.

As the pain in my chest subsided, so did my cries until a stoic face remained.

"Please, talk to me. I'm here for you," Veron implored with worried eyes.

"He…" My voice broke and I turned away. I couldn't speak. The image of the man dying before me, the reminder of the family he'd left behind without saying goodbye, it was all too much.

Recognition filled Veron's eyes. "I heard about the merman who died on the trip. I also heard you responded first, but it was too late. Hey." Veron leaned forward to see my face. "There was nothing you could have done." She squeezed my arm.

A lump formed in my throat. "I just…" I paused as more tears welled up. It was absurd that I was crying over this a week later. But every time I closed my eyes at night, all I could see was the man's gaping face. The way his mouth hung open, like a silent scream, while his face turned gray as death claimed him. I'd shake him, try to call for help, but no one came. He never responded in the dream either. His arm would remain outstretched, pointing at nothing until his eyes glassed over. I was scared to admit how much it affected me, so I kept it to myself.

He was the first person I had ever seen die. I was present when my parents disappeared, but I didn't see them die. My mind attacked me with imaginary images of my parents' faces warped in the same agony as they drowned beneath the waves.

Veron sat in silence, her hand rubbing my back, patiently supporting me.

I took a breath. Death was silence, both for those who were gone and for those left behind. I didn't know if I could talk about it. But if not with Veron, then who?

A few moments passed.

"He died," I whispered.

"I know."

"He died, and there was nothing I could do…again," my voice cracked.

"It's not your fault."

"Something so simple killed someone. One day, someone is there, and the next they're not." My lower lip trembled.

"It's part of life."

"Random death? Great. What about being turned into a mermaid? What about being attacked by a goblin shark? What about having someone you trust not trust you? What about being hunted in the streets, assaulted, and feeling totally helpless? What about losing everything you have ever known without a single hope of getting that life back?" I spiraled, putting my face in my hands as my head pounded.

"Breathe, Billie, breathe. It will be okay. I promise. Yes, life is full of surprises. Honestly, life can really suck sometimes. However, that's also how new beginnings happen, new experiences, new choices, new paths…" Veron looked out the window. "Life will always have its ups and downs, no matter how hard we try, and the unexpected is what can hurt the most. But you're strong. You are so incredibly strong, and if anyone can fight like hell to get the most out of this life, out of this world, it's you."

I peered over at Veron, who was smiling at me.

"Thanks." I wrapped my arms around her.

"Always."

"So, what are you doing here?" I changed the subject. I could process what Veron had said later.

"Are you sure you're okay?" Her brows furrowed with concern.

"Fight like hell, right?" I gave a pained smile.

Veron nodded with a smile of her own. "Fight like hell. I came to give you this." Handing me a piece of paper, she said, "Meet me here tomorrow. It's time you got out of this room a little more."

Joxpepψ, the engraved language read, etched into the stone above the archway.

I scanned the pamphlet that Veron had given me the day before.

This was the place.

I folded the flimsy algal paper and tucked it into my bathing suit top.

I pressed my hands against the bulky wooden door, and with a flick of my tail, pushed it open.

It slid open smoothly without a sound, revealing shelves full of scrolls and books. My eyes widened in awe of the spectacle rising hundreds of feet into the air.

The room had a circular appearance, and the bookcases sat on the ground creating rows to sift through, but as the area raised higher into the cavern, the cases dissipated and rows for the texts were carved directly into the walls that spiraled up to the ceiling.

Murmuring voices pulled my gaze back down. I winded through the aisles of books, meandering toward the voices while running my hand along the hand-sewn spines.

How To Kelp Weave, Tales of Tails, Sirens to Sirenians, Medicinal Properties of Sea Plants, the variety of ocean related topics were endless.

At the end of one aisle was a bucket filled with rolled paper.

I pulled one out, careful not to rip the paper as I unfolded it.

A map of the world covered the material, meticulously drawn with intimate details of the ocean currents. The land masses were drawn much smaller than on human maps, but the general shapes remained the same. In the vastness of the oceans were the names: *Erjelroze, Olboel, Mezocoe, Epzroze.* In smaller bodies of water and along coasts were smaller words scribed in the foreign language too. But my eyes were drawn to the main four.

I traced my fingers over the names sprawled in the wide expanses of the page. I had no idea how to even begin pronouncing the names of the oceans.

Wrapped around each word and spreading across the entire water were arrows. They showed the giant gyres of each ocean, major currents, as well as the local currents near coastlines with immense detail. That was why the countries were so small—to create enough space for this detail.

"Stop it!" a female voice rang out.

Brought back to reality, I refolded the map, placed it back in its home, and headed toward the commotion.

Peeking around a book stack, I watched Gavin hold a scroll above Veron's head with her hands reaching up in protest.

"Give it back," Veron whined.

Gavin smirked before bopping her on the head with the tip of the paper, and thrusting it back above his head as Veron grabbed at the empty water.

Veron grumbled before launching herself up through the water column to claim it back.

Gavin flipped backward, making a circle to swim beneath Veron, so their positions had been flipped.

Veron twirled around with a glower at Gavin, who had the scroll safely tucked behind his back.

"That's not fair." Veron flicked her tail in a way that reminded me of a child stomping their foot.

"Life's not fair." Gavin chuckled at his sister's annoyance. "Maybe if you worried less about fashion and trained a little more, you would have gotten this back already." His mocking tone permeated the water as he tilted his head to the side waving the scroll side to side, waiting for his sister's next move.

With an angry scream, Veron lunged at her brother, but he swiftly moved to the side, causing her to head straight for the ground. With a quick flip of her tail, she turned in the last second, centimeters from the bottom.

With a red face and pursed lips, she slunk to the sand with arms crossed over her chest.

I giggled, which caused them both to turn toward me.

Gavin's face drained, and he quickly tossed the scroll into Veron's lap.

Veron stuck her out tongue as she wrapped her hand around the prize.

"Sorry to…interrupt." I attempted to stifle my laughter.

"No, you got here just in time. Or my brother would have

gotten a pummeling from me. Really you saved him," Veron responded, rising from the ground with unfounded confidence.

"If you were a little faster, you wouldn't have needed my help in the first place," I teased, letting them know how long I'd been there for.

"Hey!" Veron's jaw dropped. "You're supposed to be on my side!"

I shrugged, and noticed Gavin now wore a lopsided grin.

His blue locks waved through the water as he chuckled, sending a baritone note through my chest.

My attention roamed from his broad shoulders to his muscular torso, and back up to the dark eyes that were still locked on me. A flutter went through my stomach as my face heated, causing me to look away.

What was that?

I mustered the courage to look back up.

His face was serious once more as he swam toward a table with open books strewn across it.

"I'm glad you found the place," Veron cut in as she swam over to me, grabbing my hand and pulling me toward the desk.

"Your directions helped," I said.

Veron gave me a thumbs up as she placed the scroll over the table.

The scroll unrolled slightly, and I saw *Abyssal* written across the top before the word disappeared into the rest of the fold.

I leaned over Veron to peer more closely at the paper, but Gavin snatched it away and dumped it into a basket behind him.

"Not what we were looking for," he said.

"What are we looking for?" I perused over the remaining texts. Some I could read, but most were in the unknown language I kept seeing.

My hand skimmed across the words. "I don't recognize this language. What is it?"

"Ancient mer," Veron said beside me.

I raised my eyebrow. She needed to explain a little more than that because I had no idea what she was talking about.

"It's a dead language of the merpeople." Gavin added, tracing the first line of the paragraph. His finger brushed against my hand.

We froze.

His body was rigid and his jaw set, as he glanced toward his sister.

I followed his gaze to Veron, who was too preoccupied sifting through the pages of a book to have noticed anything. I turned back to Gavin again whose serious face was already on me.

His mouth was set in a thin line and he shifted awkwardly in the water.

I frowned, pulling my hand away from the book. Did he really hate humans that much?

With a scowl, Gavin moved farther down the table. "It's what all merpeople once spoke, a unified language." He continued his explanation as though nothing had happened. "But it died out, and we only find written forms of it. Now different clans speak different languages, so most of our writings are in those languages. Only older artifacts will still be written in ancient mer."

I nodded along, the tension in my body still making it hard to speak.

"Oh! Gavin, is this it?" Veron thrust an open book at Gavin.

His eyes scanned the content, and he nodded. "Yeah, this looks familiar. My ancient mer is a bit rusty, but I'm pretty sure."

"What is it?" I sidled closer.

"I convinced Gavin to help me find the poem he would recite to me when we were kids. I couldn't find it myself."

"Can I see it?"

Gavin passed the book over to me, keeping his hand on the furthest corner of the book.

As I skimmed over the flowing script, Gavin's voice vibrated through the water, reciting it from memory.

Toj' uc terip,

toj' uc quaj.

Zψfelgi aq toj' alori

elb e dψpier ruj' xψpold.

Büm torfol fiepψr

E qψfebut torfol joiq.

Teqψf eteψ meol uc meqψr

Ol up'bip ru xidol edeol.

"What does it mean?" I asked in awe.

"The will of the water, the will of the soul. Change will unite us and bring a great toll. Deep within the heart, a shadow lies within. Wash away the pain of the past, in order to begin again." Veron added with eyes closed, a small smile toying across her lips.

"You remember?" Gavin shot her a surprised look.

"Of course. Anytime I was sick, or I had a nightmare, you were always there and would recite this poem. You'd repeat it over and over, in ancient mer and its translation, until I'd fall asleep." She smiled warmly at her brother.

He tilted his head, a gesture he only seemed to do with Veron, and his lips quirked upward.

I shoved a strand of hair from my face. "It's beautiful. But I don't understand what this has to do with anything or why you told me to meet you here."

Veron leaned over and flipped the page to the backside.

Drawn across the page were smooth lines of an androgynous human on land, crouched on the edge, looking down into the water, and a mermaid looking up from beneath. Underneath, the next picture was the human and mermaid twirled around each other in a tight embrace under the water. The tail of the mermaid wrapped gently around the legs of the human. The final marking was a final drawing of a mermaid with her hands clutched over her heart as she looked up to the top of the page.

I blinked in surprise. It was beautiful. I mean, nothing like the experience I had. This picture glorified the experience a little bit, but what story didn't do that? No one would be able discount the emotion brimming from the image, which welled in my chest. It was a mixture of pain, freedom, ending, and a new beginning. There was a balance within the artwork, which left me without words.

"Can I hold onto this?" I asked.

"Sure." Veron shrugged, and Gavin nodded his head.

He grabbed a pile of books from the table, and rose to the shelves higher in the cave. "We should put the rest of this away."

"Ugh, I hate putting the books away. It's even worse than finding them." Veron slumped as she reached for a stack of books.

Placing my new item on the corner of the table, I reached for a pile of scrolls. "I can help too."

Floating back down, Gavin frowned. "Do you even know where anything goes?"

"Well, no," I pouted. "Doesn't mean I can't learn."

"Do you even know how to read some of these texts?" He held up a spine that read *Kip uh Foq'rupoe.*

"Clearly I don't read ancient mer." I pressed my mouth into a hard line. That was a stupid question that he knew the answer to, but he didn't need to patronize me.

"You can't read it. It makes it difficult for you to help," Gavin shook his head before swimming off with more books.

"You don't need to be such a bozh," Veron yelled after him.

I cocked my head at her.

Her sheepish grin was understanding enough, but she still explained. "It's kind of like pacha but a little more…"

"Vulgar," Gavin finished for her before hitting her on top of the head with another scroll.

"You're just proving my point!" she hollered at him before pounding the water with her tail toward the bookshelves.

Reopening the book, I stared at the words across the page as they finished putting the materials away. I was in awe at what merpeople were able to accomplish under the water.

Everything in this entire library was handwritten. I wasn't sure if these were all originals or had to be rewritten with time, but the ink of this page had faded from the usual black color to a dark tan. Hours of work must have been put in to create every text, but upkeep of all the knowledge and stories it possessed must be a whole other ordeal.

With the book under my arm, I followed Veron and Gavin toward the entrance and stopped just shy of it. "Can I talk to you, Gavin? Just for a moment." I gave Veron a wane smile at the allusion I wanted a private conversation.

Picking up on it right away, Veron shot me a grin. "I have some errands I need to take care of. I'll see you around." With a quick wave, she left the library, being careful to fully close the door behind her.

Gavin turned and looked pointedly at me, arms crossed and waiting for me to speak.

I fumbled, picking at my nails, reluctant to meet his gaze.

"Well?" His tone was brusque.

That was all I needed to light the fire inside me. "Why do you hate me so much?" My hands flexed as I took in his shocked face.

He leaned back against the wall, his lips thinning in a thoughtful way as he gazed at me.

"Well?" I mimicked, matching the tone he had used earlier.

His jaw clenched, and he exhaled, then unfolded his arms. "I don't hate you, Billie."

I cut in before he could say more. "You act like it. All you ever do is remind me that I'm nothing but a lowly human who is incapable of doing anything in this world."

"You are incapable of doing things in this world," he replied as though it wouldn't be offensive.

"Are you kidding me?" I scoffed. I swam over to him until I was inches away from his face. "Just because I'm learning doesn't mean I'm incapable. Maybe you should put effort into teaching me things instead of just assuming I'm some stupid human who can't do anything. Ever thought of that?"

His lips twitched in what looked almost like a smile. Was he laughing at me? First, he admits that he thinks I'm helpless and now he was finding the idea of helping me funny?

"Seriously?" I fumed.

"Can you calm down for a second?"

"You did not just say that." I almost laughed as the fire continued to blaze inside me. "When has that ever worked for anyone? Oh, now that you pointed that out, I'm suddenly overcome with a calm ease. Thank you so much for your words of wisdom because I'm too idiotic to do it myself."

"Bad word choice, I'm sor—"

"I have done nothing but try to understand your world, and you've done nothing to try to understand mine. I give up!" I threw my hands in the air and turned to the door to leave.

His hand clasped around my wrist, spinning me back toward him.

Not expecting the momentum, I bumped into him, my hand landing on his bare chest to steady myself.

His eyes twinkled with amusement.

With my face burning, I pulled my hand from his grasp and moved back a little to create space between the two of us.

"Is it my turn?" Betraying my annoyance and embarrassment, his calm voice soothed my nerves.

I gave a curt nod, but refused to meet his gaze. Although in my peripheral vision, his head was cocked with a light smile.

"You're right."

My head shot up, and I gaped at him.

"Wait, let me finish." He ran a hand through his wispy blue hair. "I should have made more of an effort, both to help you understand my world and to try to understand where you've come from. However," his magnetic eyes flashed, "I do not feel bad sheltering you. Not everyone here is your friend, Billie. Not everyone agreed to let you live among us."

"I know that," I said, thinking back to the meeting with the mermen in the alley.

His eyes narrowed, silencing me, and he continued. "I am not doing this because I don't think you can. I am trying to protect Oceanus, Veron, you, my mother, my father…" He trailed off with a shake of his head. His shoulders tightened with the breath he held.

"Then why wouldn't you let me help with the books? I could have carried a stack or put them in piles. I mean, are you afraid that the books hate me and will crush me in their wrath?" I couldn't hold back my sarcasm, and I expected Gavin to bite back, but I still couldn't help myself.

Instead, he chuckled.

Startled by the sound, I couldn't help but smile too.

"No." His eyes bored into me until nothing else existed. "Everything will come with time, Billie. I promise."

The way he said my name sent shivers down my spine. "What exactly are you promising?"

His stoic face gave no hints about the thoughts crossing his mind as the silence lengthened. Finally, he sighed, "I promise I will do better. I will be more mindful of your ways, and of teaching you ours. Does that work?"

"Seems like a pretty open-ended promise."

"I don't want to make a promise I can't keep."

After contemplating with my lip between my teeth, I nodded and stuck out my hand. "Deal. But only if you promise never to tell me to calm down again."

He smirked. "Deal." His hand enveloped mine as we shook, causing an uninvited tickle in my belly.

TWENTY-TWO

"**E**veryone in our society contributes, as you know." Gavin was keeping his promise, teaching me the ways of Oceanus.

I just hadn't expected it to begin the next day.

We paddled through the water above the town. He had pointed out key features to me, such as the city square, the main market, and the residential area.

My gaze drifted to an area on the edge of town he hadn't brought up, but I hadn't had a chance to ask about it yet.

Gavin prattled on. "What you may not realize is that everyone finds their specialty."

I perked up, listening more intently.

"Just like humans, merpeople aren't good at everything. We often have to try multiple areas before landing on one where we feel successful or find interesting enough for us to take the time to learn."

"Wow, comparing yourself to humans in a positive way," I jested with a teasing grin.

Gavin rolled his eyes, but a hint of a smile graced his lips. "What I'm trying to say is that water collecting didn't come easily for you. If you enjoyed it, you can keep practicing until you get better, or you can try other skills until you find one that resonates with you."

We veered to a sandy building below with wide windows to allow the current to bring fresh water into it.

"I figured we could try kelp weaving today," he said.

"We?" I poked my head in the window and saw the merpeople inside knitting large strands of kelp fronds into varying garments: bags, shirts, hair wraps, carpets, and other things.

Gavin pulled up beside me. "Yes, we. I'm always looking for new ways to expand my contributions to Oceanus."

I peered up at him. "You don't know how to kelp weave?"

He shook his head. "I've never had time. I'm usually too busy helping run our defense forces or with council duty. But learning these tasks is a great way to connect with the people I aim to protect and help." His dark eyes glistened as he took in the merpeople hard at work. It was easy to see how much he cared about his people.

A piece of me warmed to him in a way I hadn't before. I was so used to seeing his rigidness, but understanding this side of it, how it stemmed from the love of his community, was beautiful.

"You came!" A merman with long turquoise hair wrapped by woven kelp into a low ponytail clapped Gavin on the back.

Gavin returned the gesture with a smile. "Nix, thanks for the invitation. How could I refuse?"

Nix was in his early thirties, which was noticeable by the minute crow's-feet in the crease of his eyes when he grinned back. "When I heard you were scouring town looking for new ways to help, how could I not?"

I widened my eyes. "You what?"

When had he found time to do this between last night and this morning? It wasn't even mid-day yet. Did he do this for me?

Gavin ran his hand through his blue locks, hiding his face with his arm.

Nix glanced between the two of us. "Let's get you two started! There's no lack of supplies to be made." He shuffled us inside. "Here we make many of the cloth-like material needs for Oceanus. We have different stations, and a newbie can really start anywhere, but I would suggest something simple like a scrub or mat."

I nodded along, absorbing as much as I could. It was fascinating how much the merpeople of Oceanus worked together. It never ceased to amaze me. I was used to the idea of working for money or clout, not because of the goodwill to contribute to the community.

He pointed to the different stations, as well as where to find materials. Some mers worked together in an assembly line formation, while others' fingers moved intricately to create pieces of artwork from scratch all by themselves.

I stopped and ogled a woman in the corner who was making intricate carpets by herself. Her fingers switched between picking up different colors of kelp from the table, to weaving them into varying patterns that seemed random at first, but soon depicted scenes. Her woven kelp masterpieces rivaled any painting I'd ever seen. "You made Edmound's carpet," I murmured in awe.

The woman paused to look at me. "Edmound?"

"Big guy, orange hair, a laugh that could shake the walls," Gavin explained as he swam up beside me to see what I was staring at.

"Ah, yes. It was a piece he commissioned for his anniversary with his wife. Very sweet family." The mermaid smiled and refocused on the project in front of her, finishing off the turtle shell design. "Speaking of families, how is yours, Gavin?"

"They're doing as well as can be expected, Marion. Thanks for asking," he replied.

She nodded. "If you need any more tethers, let me know."

I raised an eyebrow at him.

Gavin gave Marion a hard stare, but she worked away, unbothered by his menacing look.

"Marion's the best we have," Nix chimed in from my other side, causing me to jolt. "If anyone can teach you to kelp weave it's her."

"Don't go spreading those rumors again," Marion chuckled. Her lingering smile proved she enjoyed the compliment and knew what he said was true.

"Honest." He crossed his heart. "She taught me everything I know."

"I'd love to learn," I blurted. A blush crept to my cheeks when their three pairs of eyes turned on me. "If you don't mind, that is."

"Gavin, pull up a chair for the girl. And bring one for yourself!" Marion demanded.

"Yes, ma'am," he said.

Once seated, Marion got to work explaining the technique of choosing the correct strands for different products.

Use the thicker stalks for handles, straps, or the base to wrap the fine fronds around. The fronds were also great for blankets and clothes. Beginning weavers started with flat weaves, useful for bags and hair wear, but hand-hooking was better for carpets and clothing. By the time she began explaining the different species of kelp and when to use which type, my brain was mush.

"Got it?" she asked.

"I think so." Gavin picked at the buckets of kelp, and progressed right to the intermediate stage of hand-hooking.

Marion oversaw his technique, making small adjustments and suggestions, until he was weaving as quickly as the rest of the merpeople in the joint.

"Have you done this before?" I narrowed my eyes at him.

"Ha!" Nix cut in. "Mr. Spear and Fist slumming it with us weavers? No way."

"Your turn, dear." Marion gestured for me to pick from a pile of kelp fronds. "Go on, give it a try."

I picked up four long strands, and practiced a beginner flat weave.

"No, not like that. If you pull it—" Marion stopped when I did exactly what she was warning me about.

I pulled it, and the frond snapped. "Sorry," I mumbled.

"It's okay. Try again," she encouraged.

This time I placed the intricate pieces on the table for added support so I could focus on how hard I worked the fronds. They were delicate like a leaf, not as sturdy as yarn, at least until they were woven together. Once woven, they were tough like rope.

I frowned down at the fronds. It didn't look right.

"You made a knot." Marion clucked her tongue. Her eyebrows scrunched while trying to decipher where I went wrong. "Ah, I see. Go over, under, swoop, under, over. Not over under after the swoop."

"Right," I said, too embarrassed to admit I had no clue what she meant.

Marion must've seen I was still confused because she pointed, speaking the words more slowly so I could follow along. "Got it?" she asked.

"I think so," I muttered. I peeked over at Gavin, and he had finished a small rug, and had moved onto a shirt. Pursing my lips, I refocused, intent on getting this right. I would prove I could hold my own.

After another few minutes, an even larger lump sat on the table.

Marion leaned forward with scrunched eyebrows. "You really did a number on this kelp. Hmmm…I don't think we can salvage these strands. Here," she passed me some smaller pieces, "try these."

Tears pricked my eyes as I tried once again.

Marion worked beside me, weaving beautifully without even looking at her fingers while she watched my progress. Before I made a mistake, she'd stop and correct me.

Eventually, I made a flatter piece of…something. I would have considered it a napkin, but there were gaping holes in some places and tight knots in others.

Great, one more thing I failed at.

"Sorry," I whispered. I was supposed to be proving to everyone I could be an asset, proving to Gavin I wasn't a lost cause…proving to myself I could belong. Yet, here I was wasting precious material that someone undoubtedly had to risk going near shore to collect and wasting Marion's time.

Marion patted my hand. "It's okay, dear. Keep practicing, you'll get it."

"Yeah," I said to appease her, but we both knew this was a failure.

"Marion," Gavin interrupted. His eyes hardened as he looked at the hand that had touched me. "How long?"

Marion didn't answer.

"How long?" he repeated through clenched teeth.

Marion pulled her hand away and waved it in his face. "It's nothing, dear."

Black tendrils marked the skin on the back of her hand, branching out like a tree to flow inside the veins in her wrist.

"Nix!" Gavin shouted.

"What's going on?" I asked.

"Nothing," Marion repeated. "Gavin is being a worrywart."

"What is it?" Nix swam over to us.

Gavin jutted his chin toward Marion. "Her hand, how long has it looked like this?"

Nix followed his gaze. "I don't know," he gasped. "Marion! Why have you been hiding this?"

"It's nothing," she said again, but her voice was weaker, less convincing.

"What's going on?" I tried again.

Gavin peered at me. His eyes blazed with concern. "I'm sorry, but I need to deal with this."

"Is there anything I can do?" I worried my bottom lip between my teeth.

He shook his head. "Do you think you can find your way back to the castle?"

I gave him an 'I'm not stupid' look. "Swim up and look for the giant building? I think I can manage that."

He nodded, too serious to be annoyed with me like he normally would. "Nix, let's go."

Marion frowned. "I don't want to go."

Gavin placed his hands on her shoulders, and turned her toward him so he could look into your eyes. "I'm so very sorry. But it's for the best."

"I understand," Marion choked out.

They all rose, and Nix began leading Marion away.

She turned around, eyeing her table with a sorrowful frown, while Gavin's gaze bore into me.

I traced my fingers along the edge of her unfinished carpet.

TWENTY-THREE

I stared at myself in the algae encrusted mirror. Veron had dropped off a box earlier before leaving for the day with no explanation.

Inside the box was a mulberry colored *dulse* seaweed woven top. It wrapped around my torso three times to be pinned with seashells on the side. It showed off my midriff, which had become leaner from all the swimming I had done since becoming a mermaid. The deep, reddish purple of the top brought out the blue that continued to darken in my hair. My sun-driven highlights had turned a dark blue to match my tail.

I folded my bikini top and placed it in the top drawer of the dresser.

A knock came at the door.

"It's time for the King Tides festival!" Veron burst inside, grabbed my hands, and spun us around the room.

My eyebrows shot to my hairline as I flopped onto my bed with the room spinning.

"It's when the ocean has the highest and lowest tides of the year. All of Oceanus throws a huge festival during the King Tides to celebrate the life the ocean has provided us. It's so much fun." Veron beamed, bouncing onto the bed beside me.

"I was curious about that, but I'm even more surprised that you know how to knock," I taunted with a grin.

Veron rolled her eyes. "I didn't want to come in if you were dressing. That'd be rude."

"I'm glad you would find that rude instead of any of the other potential times I could have been indisposed," I continued to tease.

"You didn't have any other clothes before. This top looks fabulous on you by the way! I mean, wow!" Veron whistled.

"Whatever." I rolled my eyes and blushed.

Veron was dressed in a green seaweed top that had been embroidered with colored pearls—blue, green, pink, and black. The colors brought out her eyes.

"You look great too!"

"Thanks, I have been waiting all year to wear this. I decided not to go quite as flashy for you since you seem to get enough attention as it is," Veron added, pressing her tongue between her teeth in a quirky grin.

"Don't you get enough attention as the daughter of one of the leaders of Oceanus?" I asked.

"Yes, but I don't mind being the center of attention. I'm hoping a cute merperson will ask me to dance," she giggled.

"Dance?" I gulped.

"Yes, there's food, games, shows, and dancing!"

"What's mer music like?"

"We mostly just have the melodies. Humans use words in their songs a lot more than we do," Veron explained.

"How can you connect to it without words?" What I loved most about Carole King or Ella Fitzgerald's music was the lyrics, and how they could connect with you.

"With your body of course!" Veron gave her body a little wave, starting at her tail and moving up to her hands above her head.

I laughed as Veron continued to shimmy in a circle around me, moving her hips side to side.

"Don't worry, I'm here to help you out," Veron enthusiastically said.

"I think I'll leave the dancing to you and those cute merboys who'll be all over you," I winked.

Veron smiled. "If you say so! You never know what'll happen during the King Tides! Apparently, it's a full moon tonight too! The moon controls the ocean, the tides, and the creatures within it. Who knows what crazy voodoo will come over you. You could become the dancing queen of the night!"

"Yeah, I'm sure," I said with sarcasm lacing my voice.

A bang sounded in the distance. Outside the window, a fizzle of green light flurried through the water column, some falling back to the seafloor and other pieces drifting away with the current. Again, something shot out into the water column, and with a bang, orange flurries covered the city.

"You have fireworks?" My mouth dropped. As a child, I had always loved to see fireworks with my parents.

"In a way. We use bioluminescent microorganisms like we do with our lights, but mixed with different chemicals to get different colors," Veron explained as her face reflected the purple from another firework. "We call them luminbangs."

I gazed out over Oceanus, relishing in the wonders that continued to amaze me.

"We'd better get going. If the luminbangs are going off, it's in full swing. We can't miss the best part." Veron grabbed my hand, and instead of pulling me to the door, we left via the window and headed straight for the city square where the luminbangs were being set off.

"Squid on a stick! Get your squid on a stick!"

"Shuck your own pearls to learn your future!"

"Homemade kelp quilts, 10 percent off for the next hour!"

"Sour sea jellies! Guaranteed to pucker your mouth like a goldfish!"

"Pufferfish pop! Have a good time with some pufferfish! Must be eighteen years or older to buy!"

"Sea star hairpieces, seashell tops, sea urchin bracelets, and seashell earrings!"

"Try a free sample of smoked scallop! Just the way the humans like it!"

Vendors littered the streets with their stalls, selling clothes, food, business services, home goods, and everything in between.

I whirled around, watching as people swam throughout the water column. The meandering merpeople were closer to the ground, while the fast lane ran about twenty feet above the crowds. It was a very different atmosphere than the last time I'd been to town.

Despite the crowds, everyone was graceful, flicking their tails to easily avoid others. They twisted and turned their bodies around one another as though Oceanus was doing a choreographed dance.

That is, everyone except me.

"Watch it!" An old man with a blue-gray beard down to his belly button barked.

"So sorry," I replied, struggling to look ahead instead of at the stalls to the side.

"Oh! This would be beautiful on you!" Veron held up a sea glass necklace.

The sea glass was refined into small beads alternating between blues, greens, and purples, which landed on a piece of abalone shell that had been hand carved into a sea turtle. It reminded me of the sea turtle I had tried to save from the net.

"I don't know how I'd buy it," I said.

"That's okay! I can buy it for you!" Veron chirped, whipping out a maroon bag.

"You have currency?" I asked.

Veron dumped a pile of glass tokens into her hand. They were a variety of colors and sizes, but all stamped with a cursive O that had a fluke in the center.

I raised a quizzical eyebrow.

"They're called globus and are the currency of the ocean. The green is one globus, the blue is ten globus, and the clear is twenty globus. There is also a red globus which is fifty. We use the hydrothermal vents and melt the sand into glass, adding colors from different minerals," Veron explained as she picked through the glass.

"Can't anyone make them?" I knew hydrothermal vents were found all over the ocean, and sand definitely was, so what was stopping others from making it.

"That's what the Oceanus emblem is for. We used lava to heat metal into only a handful of stamps that are kept in a secure part of the palace. There is no way for someone to copy it. That is how we know it's legitimate."

I picked up a smooth green globus to investigate it further. Inside the fluke stamped on the glass were two small crowns. The detail was so immaculate it would be incredibly difficult to copy outside of the original creator.

"That is a very pretty necklace." An old mermaid with a shawl covering her faded green hair swam from behind her stall. "Usually it is one hundred globus, but I will sell it to you for eight-five." Her eyes sparkled at Veron, reeling her in like a fish on a hook.

"No thanks." I grabbed the necklace out of Veron's hand and gave it back to the woman.

"But…" Veron pouted.

I pushed her away from the stall. With some quick math, I'd deduced Veron had about ninety globus. I also knew she would have spent all of her money on a necklace for me, and I wasn't going to let her do that. I did appreciate the thought though.

"How about you buy me…" I scoured the area and saw a sign

for sea bubble pops for one globus. "That." I pointed.

Veron gave a little glare.

"What? I've never had it before." I beamed.

"Sea grape flavor is the best. It's so good that my scales prickle at the thought. Let's go!" Within a moment, Veron was swimming off to the stall, leaving me in her wake.

"Would you like to know what your future has in store?" A sea hag with yellowed teeth, wrinkly skin, and a black eye patch called over to me.

"Uh, I don't have enough money, sorry," I replied.

The old woman eyed my hand, where I still held a green globus. "That'll do."

"I mean, it's not mine." I searched for Veron, but couldn't see her with the crowd swimming around.

The woman held out her leathered skin. "Come darling, don't be afraid. I won't bite." She cackled at her own joke.

I treaded over the woman, drawn for an unknown reason.

"Sit." The woman pointed to a sea sponge cushion behind her booth.

I swam over the bloated plywood counter and sat on the small pillow with my tail curled to the side.

The woman pulled out a cup filled with pieces of white, dead coral. All of them had holes where the polyps had once lived. There were round pieces, horned pieces, oval pieces, and pieces that looked like blobs. The smallest coral was the size of her thumbnail, and the largest the size of her index finger.

"Clear your mind, shake the cup, and lay it out for Miss Jonah to read to you," she coaxed.

Closing my eyes, I did as directed. I cleared my mind, tuning out the mutter of the crowd and the glow from the various lanterns, and concentrated on the light. The cool current swept across my skin. Soon, even that fell away, and I only heard my heartbeat.

I used one hand to cover the open top and shook. After a few moments, a tingle crept across my hands, moved into my arms, and joined my heartbeat. I flipped the cup for the pieces to pour onto the kelp mat. I pried my eyes open. Revealing the bustling world once more, the energy hit me like a freight train.

The woman's face soured. Her eye traced the pattern of the coral as her crooked smile became somber. Her eyes whipped up, catching me by surprise.

I couldn't look away as the single icy black eye bored into me.

"I see a red sunrise with an albatross flying in the sky and a dark ocean below. The Abyssals are coming. Be warned, child. A storm is coming, bringing with it a great toll." With that, the woman quickly scooped the pieces back into the cup, using her tail to swipe the coin off of my lap to float into her money jar on the counter.

I gaped, unsure of how to respond to such an ominous fortune. Most fortunes were generalized to be interpreted by whoever they were given to. Who cared if mine was a little darker, I didn't believe in these things anyway.

The line from the poem about a great toll flashed in my mind, and I found it odd for the same language to be used. Even with the assumption the old mermaid must know the poem, a chill lingered on my spine.

"There you are!" A voice pierced through the water.

I turned to see Veron swimming over to me with a large purple circle, about the size of a candy apple, on a stick.

"Ugh! Don't waste your money on this. It is totally wash." Veron shuffled me out of the stall, thrusting the treat into my hands.

I didn't dare tell her I had used her globus, or that I was no longer hungry. Instead, I took a bite.

The texture was similar to a candy apple, but with a sweet grape flavor and a hint of saltiness. There was a fizzle in my mouth, and I smiled at the tickling sensation on my tongue.

"Yum!" I responded to Veron's expectant look.

Veron smiled and dug into hers.

After a few more bites to satisfy Veron, I found a trash can to toss it out. It tasted great, but I wasn't in the mood.

"Veron?" I caught her attention, but was nervous to ask.

"Yeah?" Veron responded as we swam through the street.

"What are the Abyssals?" I finally asked.

Veron's tail stuttered. "Let's go to a quieter area." She led me to a courtyard off to the side of the main streets where we could sit among some sea grass.

She sighed as she folded her hands in her lap. "I only know stories from when I was a kid. Mers who worked in the palace didn't know I was listening. The Abyssals are a group of outcast merpeople who live in the open ocean."

I waited for her to continue.

"They were cast out because they did horrible things. No one really knows what. Some say they murdered their friends and families. Others say they went insane and tried to burn down the castle. I heard that they got a disease and were forced to leave or it would have wiped out every merperson in the city. It's said that the ocean transformed them. Instead of hands they have claws like a stone crab. Instead of clean scales, barnacles grow all over their tails. I heard they developed teeth like an anglerfish, and eyes like a viper fish. They can create buckets of slime from their skin like hagfish and go months without eating like a Greenland shark. Whatever the case, no one who has met them has ever lived to tell the tale. There've been merpeople who have gone to search for them, but they never come back. They are the things of nightmares, and something a merperson hopes to never come across."

I tried to swallow my jitters, remembering the purple tail I saw on the water expedition. The group had been gone when I saw that tail, and the only time I had seen a tail similar to that was on a merperson.

"The last thing that's heard is the cry of a sea hawk," Veron solemnly added.

A shiver ran down my spine. Like there wasn't enough I had to worry about already, but now there were some weird sea monsters roaming the waters. Fantastic.

"Anyway," Veron chippered as though her ghost story was over, "who knows what's real or what isn't real. All I know is they're bad news and not something you ever want to come across. But you know what's more important right now? Dancing!"

And once more, I was dragged by the hand in an unknown direction.

The music was light, lyrical, and filled with a symphony of sounds. Fishing lines had been repurposed to string harps, guitars, basses, and violins. Plastic bags had been layered to create a board similar to a bass drum, which kept the beat. Reeds had been outfitted with holes to resemble flutes. A band of fifteen merpeople orchestrated melodic tunes.

In a large circular courtyard were anemones that swayed in the current and closed and reopened as merpeople danced over the top of them. The sea fans swayed and the minnows scurried. Every plant and animal moved to the music.

My jaw dropped. I closed my eyes, listening to the tune, swaying to the sounds. I smiled.

I followed Veron into the center of people. Flicking my tail and moving my hips, I danced with my hands above my head, imitating the merpeople around me. I twirled and flipped, the water flowing through my hair. I used the momentum to whip it around and let it swirl over my shoulders. I spun in a tight circle, swimming upward and ending with a somersault back down to the ground. I hadn't realized I was laughing until Veron joined in. The momentum of the music picked up, and I looked over my right shoulder to twist, but was caught by piercing cerulean eyes.

Sipping from a coral cup with full lips was a mermaid whose hair flowed down to her belly button. Her spiral hair was made of blues and purples, mixing together like a late sunset. The colors were twisted together in intermittent braids on the right side of her head, while the left side was shaved to a light blue.

My gaze drifted to her plum colored tail, and I was taken aback by the pink scars covering her left shoulder and an empty space where an arm should be.

Her single hand lowered the glass, and she smirked.

I blushed, quickly turning my head back to Veron, who was now dancing with a young merboy.

He had short evergreen colored hair and a lime green tail. He spun her out of his arms to pull her back in again.

Veron leaned back with a giggle and moved her hips with his.

I looked around, realizing I was caught among strangers, and felt sorely out of place. Veron was having a good time, and I didn't want to bother her.

Across the way, long dark hair caught my eye.

I was about to make my way to Ashmay, another friendly face, when she shifted to the side to expose Harris in front of her. They weren't dancing, but floated close together caught up in a heated discussion.

I hoped the jerk wasn't bothering her. I knew I should go over and see if she needed help, but I hesitated, shuddering at the memory of how he had held me against the ground.

I shook my head to clear it.

No, Ashmay showed up in the nick of time to help me, and I owed her.

"Excuse me?" A husky voice interrupted my thoughts.

I spun to see twinkling blue eyes fixated on me.

The gorgeous mermaid who had caught my eye earlier held out her hand. "May I have a dance?"

My head twisted toward Ashmay, but she and Harris were nowhere to be seen.

Swiveling back around, the mermaid's gaze stayed fixated on me, still waiting patiently.

Wide eyed, I nodded and placed my hand inside her soft grasp.

The mermaid whisked me onto the dance floor, using her single arm to give me a twirl.

A slight laugh escaped me, and the woman smiled. Small dimples peaked out at the corners of her mouth.

My attention grazed the spot where her left arm used to be, following the scars running across the woman's chest. A small tendril weaved its way up her bronzed neck. It reminded me of what I saw on Gloria and Marion, but instead of jet black it was more like a reddened scar. I noticed the mermaid watching my gaze and quickly averted it.

"It's okay. I'm not ashamed of it," she said.

I looked up, getting lost in her gem-like eyes. "Uhh, so what do you do? I mean, if you do something, a job. Or for fun! It's totally fine if you don't have a job." I sputtered out. It had been a while since I flirted on any level. How did adults flirt?

The mermaid chuckled, causing her intense blue eyes to twinkle.

My heart beat faster as heat rose to my cheeks.

"You're not from around here, right? I don't remember seeing you before, and I'm *shore* I would have noticed you." One side of her lips rose into a lopsided grin. "Shore…" she emphasized before chuckling at her own joke.

Her light laugh cut into my groan, and before I knew it, I was laughing with the mermaid.

Clearly, she didn't know I was the detested ex-human or I doubt she'd be joking with me. I guess there was one benefit of my hair changing color. I didn't know if I should tell her who I was or if that would ostracize me more. I assumed everyone knew who I was, but it isn't as though I had met every merperson in Oceanus, so there was no way for them to all know me. But should I admit I was actually human, or lie and pretend I was from Oceanus?

The mermaid was still waiting for an answer.

She brushed a tendril of my hair out of my face, and the heat of the water around her hand warmed me.

It was as though giant manta rays were batting around in my stomach.

"Let's start with names."

"I'm Billie," I whispered.

"My name is Aadya." She bowed her head.

We were barely moving to the music, slowly moving side to side in unison.

Aadya placed a hand on my hip, causing my breath to catch.

Again, she smirked before her eyes looked over my shoulder and became hooded. She looked back at me, the tension diminishing from her face. "It's been lovely meeting you, Billie."

Before I could respond a voice came from behind me.

"May I cut in?"

I turned to see Gavin staring down at me.

His eyes took in all of me.

"I was dancing with…" I pointed, but Aadya had disappeared. I searched the dancing crowd but couldn't find her.

"With?" he asked.

"Uh, no one." I returned my attention to Gavin to see him softly smiling at me. "I'd love to dance." I grinned back.

His hands rested on my waist, and I returned the gesture by putting mine on his broad shoulders.

We swirled together, rising fifteen feet off the ground, to somersault away from each other and end up back where we began. Once back on the ground, our hands came together and I moved outward holding one of his hands in mine, which Gavin used to spin me back into his chest.

He grinned down at me, the sharpness of his jawbone accentuated as waterworks burst in the sky above them.

Yellow fluorescent specks floated around us like we were surrounded by stars. The back of his hand grazed my cheek.

I pulled away with a mischievous grin, and swam in a circle

around him.

He spun in the opposite direction like he was trying to catch me, making a small whirlpool of energy.

We stopped swimming, allowing the mini waterspout to continue our movement.

Gavin moved into a pencil formation, allowing himself to spin faster, and I let the water make my body move in slow circles. As the water died down, we ended back in front of each other, breathing heavily.

I placed my forehead on Gavin's broad chest.

He circled his arm around my back.

I peered up into his dark eyes.

His chest rose as he took a deep breath. He opened his mouth, ready to say something, when a caw came from the distance.

The music stopped as another bird call echoed through the waters.

Gavin's hand pressed into my back, scouring the area.

The crowd looked around wildly.

The caw sounded again, reminding me of a hawk.

The crowd went rigid.

The old woman's voice sounded in my head, *The Abyssals are coming,* followed by what Veron had said, *The last thing that's heard is the cry of a sea hawk.*

Gavin grabbed me by the shoulders, "I need you to go back to the castle."

"What's going on?" My fingers dug into his arm.

"Go back to the castle, please." His pleading eyes bored into me.

"No. I'm staying with you. I can help," I retorted, defiantly pulling my arm out of his grasp.

He closed his eyes and took a breath as he pinched his nose. "Billie, listen, I cannot have you out here. Whatever is going on, I need to know you're safe. Please, please go back to the palace."

Already, people were rushing around, kids were crying, mothers called for their children, men ushered their families away while others banded together. The flurry of the water whipped my hair around.

"Okay," I acquiesced. My eyes swept over his tense jaw and hard eyes. "But be safe. Promise me, if there is anything I can do, you'll let me know. I want to help."

His gaze turned soft as he looked at me. "I know, but for now, the castle is the best place for you."

"Promise me."

His lips squeezed together; I knew he didn't like to make promises he couldn't keep.

"I promise." He squeezed my hand before swimming off to a group of mermen, already shouting directions as he went.

I headed for the palace in the distance.

TWENTY-FOUR

Screams could be heard all over the city. There were the high pitches of frightened children, shrill cries of worried mothers, shouts from those preparing to protect their homes, and small whimpers from those who cowered. It all blended together, creating a cacophony of chaos.

I pushed harder with my tail, willing myself to swim faster than I ever had before. I could now see the bustling outlines of merpeople in the windows of the palace. The seaweed curtains flapped outside of my bedroom. The current had picked up with the pandemonium enveloping Oceanus, whipping my hair to the side. I headed for my room, but stopped short when I saw a larger man giving orders to mermen and women in front of the main door.

"Edmound, what're you doing here? Shouldn't you be with your family?" I hustled between the crowd amassed with spears, spikes, spear guns, and harpoons.

Edmound's stern face swept across me, bushy eyebrows drawn together. "My wife is a very capable woman. I have full faith that she can protect my family. There is no one better suited in these seas than her to protect those she loves," he chastised.

Regret wormed its way through my intestines. Just because he was a guard didn't make his wife any less capable of protecting Oceanus. "I'm sorry, Edmound. You're right. What can I do to help?" I squared my shoulders, ready for him to hand me a weapon of my own.

He sized me up, shoulders slumping as he sighed, and placed a hand on my shoulder. "Billie, I appreciate ye willin'ness to protect our city. But yer just not ready, lass. My wife was in the guards before me and only stopped once we had the littles. She has a helluva aim and I've seen her swim fifteen miles at top speed without stoppin' for a break. I don't mean this to be harsh, but yer still gettin' yer fin about ye. Yer a guppy in comparison to the rest of us. So for now, go inside, and stay safe. Someone will find ye when it's over."

A lump the size of a clam shell formed in my throat. No matter what I did, I didn't fit in. I no longer had a home on land, and I didn't belong here either. I had lost my sense of home when I lost my parents, and I feared it would never return.

I batted away the tears forming in the corner of my eye, and nodded at Edmound, wishing him good luck, before turning away to head inside. I would sit and wait in the castle, the only thing anyone thought I was good for.

Once inside, the havoc was no more subsided than out in the streets. Everyone rushed around, creating circular currents that pushed me around despite never being bumped by a single merperson.

Still determined to be helpful, despite my torn pride, I set off to find someone who would take me seriously. I refused to sit in my room and do nothing. Preparing meals for those who were out of the front line, setting up a triage area in case someone got hurt, helping to barricade doors and windows, my head swam with worst case scenarios. I was ready to support Oceanus in whatever way they would allow.

Sadly, the merpeople I came across were already so driven, they swam past me without a single glance. Trying to get someone's attention would definitely be more of a hindrance than a help to them. I roamed the halls, looking for someone, anyone, who was not in a rush. That was easier said than done.

"What have I done? What have I done?!" A crash echoed through the empty halls.

I hadn't seen anyone for about five minutes, and was on the verge of giving up hope. The commotion was almost a welcome sound.

I swam to a bloated wooden door with iron woven into thick bands across the threshold, creating a layer of support and added strength. I eased open the door.

A bioluminescent globe lay in shattered pieces in the corner, the flecks escaping into the open water. There were no windows, so they had nowhere to go but to spread through the room creating a star-like appearance. Paper littered the large room.

A man hunched in the corner, his dark blue tail curled beneath him. His hands covered his face and his long white-blue hair covered his hands as his body shook.

"Raiden?" I crept toward him. "Are you okay?"

"What have I done?" he repeated to himself.

"Don't worry, there's plenty of mers taking care of it." I drifted closer, not wanting to startle him. "Do you remember me? I met you at my trial. I'm Billie." I reached for his shoulder.

His hand shot out, grabbing me by the wrist and causing pain to shoot up my arm.

I gasped.

The tendrils of his hair wisped out of his face to reveal wild eyes darting around the room. His hand, the size of a baseball mitt, squeezed harder, holding almost half my forearm.

My fingers turned white and my radial bone ached from the pressure.

"Raiden…you're…hurting…me," I said through gritted teeth, trying to pry myself from his grip.

His eyes locked onto my face and onto where he held me. He let go. "I'm so sorry. I'm so sorry." He looked at his palm in shock, like his hand had a mind of its own.

"Are you okay?" I asked, rubbing my wrist as I slowly backed away.

"I just…" He frowned. "I'm sorry. I didn't mean to." His face contorted with an internal pain. He must've been scared out of his mind.

I was so used to merpeople being audacious, I forgot they could still feel fear too. Shaken, I swam over to the shards of the broken lamp to pick them up.

"It's okay, Raiden. I'm here to help." I dropped the pieces into the larger part of the broken globe and set it on a wooden desk likely salvaged from a shipwreck.

"This is a serious situation." Raiden paced the room, stroking his unshaven face.

"Yes, I know, that's why I'm trying to help, even though I'm scared too," I agreed.

"Scared will not help us. We must do what we must do," he continued, never taking his eyes off the ground he swam over.

"What can I do? I know I'm a new mermaid, but I have grown up around the ocean. Just because I am new to a tail doesn't mean I'm new to the sea. I can still help," I explained.

"Help isn't coming. There is no help. We must take care of this ourselves or it'll be the last of us." Raiden stopped and began rifling through the papers on the desk. As he sorted through the papers, the ones he found useless he'd scoff at before pushing them off to the side and letting them float to the floor. Finally, he stopped at one piece of paper.

I didn't want to interrupt, but it was pointless for me to float here watching him. Still, he seemed to be the only person who might give me a job once he figured out what he needed. So, I waited.

"This can't be right. This…can't be right." Raiden shook his head.

"What is it? Can I help?" I swam over to peer over his shoulder. "Is it the Abyssals? Is there something I can do?"

The name *Hedeon* was written at the top of the page he held.

"No. Why?" His voice broke as his body went rigid.

He must've found something important, something we could use to help Oceanus.

214

TWENTY-FIVE

"**B**illie, what are you doing in here?" Gavin's worried voice echoed through the room.

"I think your father found something important!" I was about to explain the paper, but within a split second, Raiden had swum over me and grabbed Gavin by the throat.

"Why would you do this?" Raiden boomed.

"Dad," Gavin choked, his face turning red.

"Tell me the truth! How could you?" Raiden screamed into Gavin's face. His knuckles tightened, covering Gavin's entire throat and blocking his airway. He pulled Gavin away from the door and held him above his head. "I said tell me!" He slammed Gavin hard into the concrete wall. Bits of sand floated down from the ceiling.

I swam over and pulled on Raiden's arm. "Stop it! You're hurting him!" I screamed.

Gavin's face turned purple; his hands pried at his father's.

"Why would you do this to us! To Oceanus!" Raiden did not let up. The water around him was close to boiling.

"Raiden! Stop it!" I cried.

A shard of glass lay on the ground.

I picked it up and held it tight. The sharp edges cut into my palm, and blood seeped into the water. I raised it above my head and drove it into Raiden's arm.

At the same time, Gavin thrust his tail against his father's chest.

Raiden wailed, letting go of his son and flying to the other side of the room.

Gavin grabbed my wrist. I winced as he held the same spot his father had earlier.

We slipped out of the room, slamming the door behind us, and raced through the halls until we could no longer hear Raiden's wails.

"Are you okay?" My body shook. What had just happened? Why would Raiden attack his own son? It was like he wasn't fully present.

Gavin hunched forward, coughing and taking shaky breaths.

My lip trembled. "Gavin?"

"Why…were you…in there?" His eyes were filled with pain. Pain from trying to talk, pain from his father's attack, and another pain I didn't understand.

"I just wanted to help. Why wouldn't I be safe with your family?" I whispered.

"I told you to go to your room," his voice croaked, ignoring my question in his usual manner, which made my mouth pucker with annoyance.

"You told me to go to the palace, which I did. But I still wanted to help."

"Well, you didn't."

Tears fell down my cheeks. "I don't understand. What happened in there? I thought he had found something about the Abyssals. I thought I was helping."

"Don't worry about it. Forget what you saw." His face was sour and bruises formed around his neck.

"How can I forget what I saw? Your father just attacked you, Gavin," I exclaimed as my vision blurred.

"It's none of your concern. It's a family thing. Please do not speak a word of this to anyone." He looked into my eyes, imploring me to leave it alone.

I hesitated, waiting for an explanation. "Fine," I conceded. He wasn't going to tell me, as usual. Why did I even try to help? To fit in? To think he would accept me? It was pointless.

"Now, will you please go to your room? We are still trying to figure out what is happening and why the Abyssals are attacking. I need to know you are safe. So go to your room and stay there. Please. Do not leave until I come to get you." He took my hands in his own as though he were trying to warm them on a cold winter morning.

My throat constricted. I really was useless.

Gavin tilted my chin up with his knuckle. Our lips were inches apart as he stared into my eyes. "I need you to listen to me. I am asking this because I care, not because I don't think you can handle yourself. You are an asset. You are meant to be here. I want you to be here."

He wanted me here. This difficult merman beside me with his icy exterior who had rarely spoken kindly of humans told me he wanted me here, and for once, I felt I could truly find a place within this world.

"For now, I need to go back out and help, and I need to make sure you aren't getting yourself into trouble. You're still learning about this world."

"Okay, but remember you promised to teach me about this world," I reminded him.

The corner of his mouth curled up. "I know. I will. But for the time being, go where it's safe."

"Fine," I agreed.

He pulled away, giving me a small nod, before swimming away from me once again.

I reached my sandy room with a sigh. I shook slightly, flashes of Raiden's hand around Gavin's neck going through my mind, the same force he had used to grab my wrist. I should've left as soon as that happened, as soon as he manhandled me like that I should've gone to my room like Gavin had asked me to. Gavin wouldn't have gotten hurt if I'd only listened.

I traced the cut on my hand. A jagged, uneven cut disrupted what was known as the life line. It started between my thumb and forefinger and severed down to the hilt of my palm. Flexing my hand and feeling the salt in the water seep into the wound, it sent a wave of pain. I hissed through my teeth, releasing the tension in my hand. It had stopped bleeding, a dark brown clot forming a scab.

How did a scab even form under water? Anytime I had a scab on land, I was banned from the water until it healed. Every time I entered the water, the wound would moisten, and by the time I left, it would be open once more, the new flesh exposed. I had plenty of scars on my legs to prove it.

My body must have heated up without me realizing, cauterizing the wound like Gavin had done for my tail.

I glanced down at it, nothing but smooth, deep blue scales mixed with black streaks shone back at me, reminding me of the bruises forming on Gavin's neck.

Yet another piece of my human life was becoming nothing more than a memory. The concave scar on my shin that once existed from me falling off a dock at night was nowhere in sight. I found it odd how the tiniest things could go unnoticed, but somehow could feel like the weight of the world once they were seen.

I deflated.

I was exhausted, this was all so much. It was like everything that had happened was finally catching up with me. All I wanted to do was curl up and fall asleep for a few weeks.

With a flick of my tail, I moved to my bed, allowing the door to shut behind me, and leaving me in mild darkness except for the light shining through the windows. I brought my tail to my chest, and wrapped my arms around to hug it. I wished my mother was here.

I lowered my forehead to my bent tail, feeling the sleekness of it, and allowed my new reality to sink in. I would give anything to go back to my silly problems.

"It took you long enough," a deep voice I recognized said from the corner.

I schooled my face before looking up to see Harris come out of the shadows. The merboy who had made me feel physically vulnerable was now invading my space to see me emotionally weak. Hell, no.

"Get out of my room. You have no right to be here!" I pushed myself from my bed, ready to confront him.

He leered as his tongue swiped over his lips. "Well, well, well. Someone is becoming more of a bull shark." He ambled over to my dresser, opened a drawer, and pulled out my bikini top. He grimaced. And dropped it back inside in disgust.

"What do you want?" I glared. My stomach rolled with nausea at his closeness.

"We want you gone. We want you to disappear from Oceanus the way you should have after your hearing," he snarled as he swam toward me.

I grabbed the base of the orb beside my bed and held it at my side, preparing to swing it at his head. The jarring movement brought the bioluminescent creatures to life, casting a blue glow across the room.

Harris cackled in response. "So tough now. You really think you can move quick enough to even hit me? You've been a mermaid for what? A month? I've been a merman for twenty years! I bet you couldn't even touch me if your life depended on it." The light shone off his dark, cruel eyes and menacing smile.

"Why don't we find out?" I prodded as I tightened my grip on the lamp. If I could fight off a goblin shark, I could take this creep.

Within a split second, Harris had closed the distance and ripped the lamp out of my hand, throwing it across the room and smashing it against the wall.

I elbowed him in the side. He doubled over, giving me the opportunity to swipe the side of his head with my tail. I backed toward the window, never taking my eyes off him. The bioluminescence flickered as they were swept out of the room with the current, casting more shadows inside.

"You're going to regret that," Harris sneered as blood seeped from his lip.

"Wanna bet?" I smirked.

A dark bag flew over my head, blocking everything in sight.

I had been so transfixed on Harris, I never even considered one of his friends might be in the room too.

I started to thrust my elbow into the merman behind me, but strong hands caught it.

The merman wrenched my arms behind my back. One hand held the bag in place, pulling it so tight that I could barely breathe. It took all my strength to pull small sips into my body, prohibiting me from screaming for help.

I was stuck.

"Son, stop squabbling with this scum and come help me."

I recognized his voice too, but no face came to mind in my panicked state.

"Now! Before this wretched human escapes and puts our plan in jeopardy!" The man barked.

I thrashed wildly. I wouldn't go down without a fight. I bucked and rammed, despite my lack of air.

Harris's hands grabbed me.

With my waning energy, and two strong mermen pinning me down, there was no way I could escape.

Then I felt the bag loosen around my neck. I gobbled in hungry breaths, helping to clear the fuzz from my mind.

All I needed was to calm down and call for help. Surely someone would hear me. Sound traveled farther in water than it did on land.

I shook my head from side to side, trying to loosen the bag further. My fin beat the water, pushing the merman behind me into the wall.

One of the mermen grabbed my tail, holding me down, while the other focused on keeping his grip on my hands.

As the bottom of the black bag lifted up, my breathing became easier. The bag floated through the water, and I opened my mouth, pulling in a breath of water. I turned my head to see who had ambushed me from behind.

"Gav—" I started to scream, seeing a tendril of black hair.

Pain shot through the side of my head and everything went dark.

$$\Psi$$

When I came to, the first thing I noticed was my throbbing head. The next was the darkness around me.

A bag was tied around my neck, but not so tight that I couldn't breathe.

"Help! Someone help!" I hollered as I attempted to move my body. The sound of my own voice pierced my skull. My eyes fluttered at the painful shock.

Pressure lanced across my body. Ropes. I was tied with no chance of freeing myself.

"It's no use. No one can hear you out here. But feel free to scream if you want to see if a shrimp will come to your rescue," Harris goaded with a malicious chuckle.

With the bag over my head, I couldn't tell which direction he was in.

"Where am I?" I asked. I continued to move against the ties until the rope burned my skin.

"Wrong question," Harris taunted.

I could envision his rat-like smirk as he said this, and it made me sick.

"Is she secure?" The other man's voice rang out.

"Of course. I used our strongest Abyssal thread rope. She isn't going anywhere," Harris mused as he grazed a finger over my left shoulder.

I tried to pull away from his touch.

"We should get out of here before they arrive," the cold voice suggested.

"Before who arrives?" I interjected.

"Still the wrong question," Harris chortled.

The water moved on my right a second before I felt his breath on my ear. I might actually spew.

"I think you should be asking what, as in, what is going to happen to you?" he whispered.

I veered my head away from him.

The ropes tightened around my shoulders, pushing my shoulder blades into something hard behind me. I was tied to some kind of plank, from my shoulders to the tip of my tail. Only my head had any kind of freedom.

"Let's go. The Abyssals will find her and take care of her, and our problem will be gone." The voice was charged with authority.

I heard the swishing of the tails, a cloud of sand dusting up around me with the tiny bits of debris hitting my skin. I waited for Harris to continue with his snide remarks, but nothing came.

"What? No goodbyes?" I mocked. Goosebumps formed across my skin.

Silence.

"Oh, come on. You always need to get the last word in," I prodded with my heartbeat quickening.

Silence.

"Harris?" I tried to wriggle my body.

Silence.

The cold current picked up, whipping the bag against my face, making me shiver, proving how exposed I was to the unknown realm.

I must be on the outskirts of town, an area leading to the deep ocean.

"Help!" I yelled. "Someone please help me! Gavin! Veron! Ashmay!"

I screamed until my throat was raw.

No one came. Nothing but the cold waters met me.

Blood trickled down my jawline. My stomach churned. What would happen if I threw up in the bag while it was tied around my face? Could I still suffocate as a mermaid?

My head lolled to the side as the adrenaline subsided in my body. Waves of pain crashed through me. The cut on my palm, the rope burn across my body, the gash where I had been hit in the head; it was all too much to bear.

Bile rose in my throat, but I swallowed it back down. Someone would notice I was gone and they would be looking for me. I just needed to hold on.

My eyes fluttered. I forced them open despite not being able to see anything. I swore there was a whoosh of a tail.

"Hello? Is someone there?" I murmured. The sound of my words felt like a ton of bricks slamming against my skull.

Silence.

The darkness closed in on my mind. I fought to stay awake, fought to wait until someone came and saved me.

My body relaxed, the pain subsided, and my senses became muffled.

The little clicks of the shrimp filling the waters sounded distant. I thought I heard the sound of crashing waves, the sound of people moving around me.

It was all so distant, but it was there.

I could feel the sun on my skin again and the sand between my toes.

I was fine. It was all okay.

A hawk called in the distance as darkness surrounded my mind.

Rising Swells, The Sirenia Chronicles

Book 2

Releasing 2022

ROGUES. POISON. DEATH.

I thought my life was over, but I was saved by The Abyssals-- a feared vigilante group of merpeople.

Oceanus was not what it seemed, and I had to learn this the hard way. My body will become my weapon; I will show everyone here that I belong. But my heart still pulls for those I left behind-- Gavin and Veron.

Do they know the truth of Oceanus? Are they a part of the plastic poisoning killing its citizens? If they do, they're not who I thought they were.

Follow me for updates.

Stay Up To Date

Keep up with new releases, special offers, giveaways, and exclusive content through any of the following:

Join my monthly newsletter:

https://www.kristenbraddock.com/newsletter-1

Join my Facebook Group:

https://www.facebook.com/groups/859119421665171/

Follow me on Instagram

https://www.instagram.com/kristenbraddockauthor/

Dear Reader

Thank you for taking a chance on Changing Tides. This was the first completed manuscript of mine, something I began in college after becoming a SCUBA diver and worked on for nine years. Through the years I became a SCUBA instructor, a marine science teacher, and received a Master's in Fisheries and Aquatic Science. The ocean has my heart, and my mind, and I hope this novel helps show that.

Creating a world based on real ocean phenomena, but had all the fantastical plot points we love in YA, was thrilling because I got to combine two passions in my life into one. I hope you enjoyed reading it as much as I loved writing it.

I'm so sorry for the cliffhanger! I know it's a bit of a doozy. Book 2 is written, and just needs to be edited, so my hope is to have it out sooner rather than later. Thank you in advance for any reviews or suggestions you make in accordance with this book. Those are a lifeline for indie authors, and taking the time to both read and write a review is greatly appreciated by me.

I am able to do what I do because of you. I have always had stories and characters in my mind, but it's you on why I keep publishing.

Kristen

Acknowledgements

A huge shout out to my beta reader, Becky James, and editor, Sara Lawson. Without your diligent feedback, I would not have been confident with publishing this book. You two took a rough, first manuscript, and helped me turn it into something I could be proud of. Thank you for all of your help and encouragement.

Thank you to Jess Grimes, my original alpha reader, for being the person that made me actually finish this novel. I admit, those nine years were on and off with writing, and my dream of being an author fell to the wayside as I got older. Without you, this book would still be in limbo and I would not have found my path as an author.

Finally, to my husband, Rudy, you are my rock. You are the reason I can not only imagine dreams, but live them. I know I can be a pain, overly focused, and get stressed easily, but you help bring sanity back into my life and make me feel like I can achieve anything I set my mind to. Thank you for your continuous love and support, it means the world to me (as do you).

Read More By The Author

Cara Winters is cursed.
Loss has haunted her through life. A fun night out with her sister ends in disaster when she learns she's a banshee. With a chance encounter and life debt owed, she's coerced into a deadly competition in the far realm. To survive she finds an unlikely ally in Killian, a mysterious and prickly dark fae.
The only way to win and get back to Earth is using her powers, but doing so may unravel her to the point of no return.

Perfect for fans of fated mates, enemies to lovers, complicated & diverse characters, slow burn romance, and celtic folklore.

10% of author profits will be donated to Foundations for Divergent Minds Organization.

SNEAK PEAK

ONE

"You're a lifesaver." I praise my sister as I curl my hand around the mug she hands me, inhaling the earthy aroma of coffee.

"I don't know how you drink it like that, Cara." Shauna grimaces as I pour my fourth container of half and half into the mug.

No sugar, all cream, and one hundred percent bliss.

"I don't know how you expect me to function when you wake me up at six in the morning to work out… without coffee," I grumble before taking a sip of the liquid gold.

She rolls her piercing green eyes, a shade lighter than my own, and a match to our mother's. "You mean the *workout* that lasted five minutes because you were too busy whining how hard it was? Or do you mean the *workout* of walking to your favorite coffee place after you gave up?"

I glare at her as she air quotes "workout."
"You wanted me to run… two miles! Run! Do you think I changed into another person overnight?" I huff as I settle into the velvet armchair in the back corner of the quaint coffee shop.

Comfortable reading chairs fill the room. Books line the walls, and the bottom half of the tables have shelves to hold more options. Plants glow in the windowsills and hang from the ceiling, morphing the area into an inside garden. The morning light drifts through the large windows, casting leafy shadows across my blue leggings.

"Woah, woah, woah. I gave you options." She takes a sip of her caramel frappuccino, and I gag at the sugar content.

"You said I could either go out tonight with you or do a workout. I don't know if those were fair options." I pout when I bring my cup to my lips to find it empty.

Shauna rubs her right temple as she leans back into her seat. "You were the one complaining how frail you are and how you have no life. I was trying to help."

"Can't a girl complain anymore without someone trying to solve her problems?" My eye snags on a waitress as she walks through the cafe with a coffeepot in hand.

Spotting my pleading look, the goddess that she is, she waltzes over to top me off.

"Keep it coming, but room for extra cream, please," I smile at her.

"Need anything else?" She asks my sister as she fills my cup to the brim.

I hold my breath as I take a couple gulps of the bitter substance, ignoring the scorch on the roof of my mouth. Three creamers later, the coffee is back to the rim of the cup.
"Is there anything you suggest?" Shauna runs her hands through her pixie cut brown hair with a smirk.

"We have fresh chocolate croissants. I made them myself," the waitress smiles as she places the pot down on the small table between us, transfixed by my sister.

"Oh, sounds delicious. I'd love one of your treats to go," Shauna winks.

The server blushes before nodding and turning away, forgetting her coffee pot.

"Keep it in your pants," I say. I top off my cup again with coffee and another container of half and half.

"Don't hate the game," she leans back with a smug look.

"Whatever." I stew at my sister's confidence because when I manage to speak to someone remotely attractive my words twist into gibberish.

"Since you didn't complete the workout, I guess that means you are coming out with me tonight." A devilish grin forms across her face, causing my stomach to instantly drop.

I cough as I choke on my coffee. "What? No! That's not fair."

"It's one hundred percent fair, Cara. You had a choice, and you didn't complete the workout, so going out it is."

"Shaun," I revert to her nickname, "I'm twenty." Heaven forbid I am at a bar past ten at night, but can give my life to serve my country. Welcome to the United States.

"So?" She casually inspects her nails.

"Are we going to an eighteen and over club?" I raise an eyebrow.

My sister looks at me in abject horror. "Absolutely not! Talk about predators galore. I'd rather sleep with a man than go to an eighteen and over club."

I snort, "I guess I'm off the hook."

"Don't you worry about that. What time are your classes over today?" Her attention drifts over my shoulder as she talks to me. No doubt appreciating our server again. The corner of her lip quirks up. Hypothesis confirmed.

"My Intro to Animal Physiology ends at six p.m." I'm in my third year of a local state university thanks to Shauna's willingness to support me while I attend school full time.

My sister shakes her head, "I still don't understand why you chose to take a Saturday class."

"It's the best local college for veterinary medicine, of course they have these kinds of classes. Plus, Saturday classes help open up time during the week for work-study programs."

"Have I told you recently how proud I am of you?" She smiles.

I wave her off. I haven't found the courage to tell her about my C on my most recent exam. "I'm barely hanging on with the scholarships as it is. I have no idea how I'll pay for graduate school," I grumble.

"That's what student loans are for!" She sticks her tongue out at me.

I turn my head, biting my inside cheek. I love animals, and after our parents died when I was eight, I dived into academics.

My sister is six years older and fought to keep us together while we bounced between foster homes, but once she turned eighteen, she adopted me. With all the inconsistencies and moving, let's just say that school became the stability I desperately needed in life. I hadn't been planning on going to university due to finances. I saw how hard my sister worked to raise me, and I wanted to get a job immediately out of high school to help out, but she wouldn't let me. She never got the chance to go to college due to raising me, so her guilt trips easily swayed me. She claimed with my grades compared to hers, I was the better choice for higher education.

Today is the first day in months she's only working one of her three jobs. She is an assistant during the day, bartender at night, and drives for a ride share company in her spare moments. She has been the one constant in my life, and I hope to return the favor one day.

"Speaking of," she drawls before slamming an envelope onto the table. "When were you going to tell me about this?" Her hand peels away to reveal a letter addressed to me, the top ripped open like it's been through a lawn mower accident.

"You know it's illegal to open other people's mail." I glare at her. I drag the contents out of the white sleeve, and my eyes widen at the words written on the page.

Dear Cara Winters,

Congratulations, you have been accepted to the Atlanta Veterinary Internship Program.

I read the first line five times until the words sink in.

"I didn't think I'd get in," I whisper. This is one of the most prestigious internships in the area, and they receive thousands upon thousands of applicants every year and only accept five.

"I'm so proud of you!" Shauna bounces in her seat like a kid on Christmas. "But still a little vexed you didn't tell me you applied."

"Vexed? Have you been binging British tv shows again?"

"What? Have you heard their accents?" She fans her face. "One day I'm going to find myself a sexy woman from the UK."

I continue to stare at the paper as my sister prattles on about her obsessions with the Brits. I can't believe I actually got in. This is almost a guarantee I will get into a graduate program; no one who has done this internship has been denied.

"Yup, definitely going out tonight to celebrate. Will your boyfriend be joining us?" Shauna waggles her eyebrows, eliciting an eye roll from me.

"How many times do I have to tell you Marcus is not my boyfriend?"

"Why aren't you two official yet? You've been dating for, like, six months! And he's a total cutie."

I shrug. "You know how it is with college boys." Shauna raises an eyebrow, and I chuckle. "Okay, well maybe *you* don't. But it's casual, nothing serious."

"Just keep it to when I'm working so I don't have to hear you're 'casual' through the walls."

"Whatever." I shake my head. "You of all people shouldn't act so innocent."

"What do you mean? I'm pure innocence." She bats her eyes and holds her hands above her head in a circle to symbolize a halo.

"I think your horns are making it a little crooked," I retort.

"Damn, I really need to do something about those things." A wide smile breaks out, and we both fall apart laughing. "Okay, well, I'm off. Since our workout ended early, I'm hoping to do a couple rides before my shift starts at the office. Be home by six-thirty to get ready. Feel free to invite your man." Shauna packs her things and throws a twenty on the table as the waitress walks over.

Okay, apparently she will be working one of her other jobs.

"Leaving already?" The server hands a white paper bag to my sister. "Here's your croissant."

"Thanks," she grabs it with a sly smile. "I'm sure I'll be back."

Again, my eyes roll. Of course she'll be back, I drag her here every other Saturday.

"Well, I guess I'll see you soon," the waitress hesitates, searching for something more to say, but a customer waves for her attention across the restaurant. "Have a wonderful rest of your day," she says.

As she walks away, my sister unabashedly checks her out.

"Excuse you!" I gape. "What if she doesn't swing that way?"

My sister grins as she tilts the side of the bag towards me. Written in black sharpie is the name Rose with a phone number underneath.

With a shake of my head, I stand and give her a hug. "See you tonight. Although six-thirty seems awfully early to get ready."

"We've got to eat and pregame, girl!" Pulling away, Shauna chuckles at my stricken face before turning to saunter out the door.

"Stupid bus," I mutter to myself. "How can anyone plan their day if busses could range anywhere from being ten minutes early to twenty minutes late?"

Even though I wasn't talking to him, Marcus still decides to answer. "Walking not only reduces our carbon footprint, but will increase our cardio and pulmonary fitness, reduce the risk of heart disease, improve management of hypertension, and improve balance."

"I don't have hypertension I need to manage," I say.

He laughs. "And thank goodness for that. Taking the bus will help keep it that way."

I glance sideways at Marcus. He walks casually beside me, a satchel slung over his shoulders containing all of his pre-med texts and hands shoved in his pockets. His short chestnut hair catches the sun, while his pale skin is covered in jeans and a jacket. He is the epitome of health, which makes sense with his determination to become a doctor. When he's not studying for his classes, he's often working out or making meals with fresh produce. He's a good looking guy, and I have no doubt I'm not the only girl he makes breakfast for in the morning. But he does a good job of not making it obvious. Not that I care, we never made what we have official.

I mull over the conversation with my sister this morning. He is a nice guy, can cook, determined, and not terrible in bed. Maybe I should try to make him my boyfriend. "Hey, Marcus?"

"What's up?" He peers down at me, a smile of perfect teeth crossing his face.

Losing my moxie, I change my question last minute. "Do you want to come out with Shauna and I tonight?"

"Oh." He massages the back of his neck while giving me an apologetic smile. "I have plans."

"Oh, yeah, no worries. It's no big deal."

"Maybe next week?"

"Yeah, sure. Sounds good."

Marcus whistles a random tune to fill the silence.

A brown leaf crunches under my foot, causing a shallow smile to creep onto my face. Despite our crisp pace, I veer under the maple trees whose autumn leaves litter the ground. I tuck my hands into my grey sweater as the leaves continue to crackle beneath my shoes.

My feet slow when I notice a jet black dog beside a tree ahead of me. No other person is nearby to claim him. Despite being an avid lover of all animals, I have always been more fond of dogs.

A sharp breeze blows, causing my dark hair to drift into my face, carrying with it the scent of autumn, chimney smoke, and sandalwood.

The dog lifts his head and sniffs the air, turning his head to stare directly at me. My mouth drops as his amber eyes seem to darken.

"Hey bud," I reach my hand tentatively towards it. "Where's your owner?" I ask as I eye his collarless neck. His thick fur shimmers in the afternoon light, and his body is lithe with muscles without showing any bones. I doubt he is a stray.

"I don't think you should do that," Marcus says from behind me.

I ignore him, and continue to coo at the dog.

He inches towards me with his head down and ears back. Unlike a barking dog with perked ears who seem more aggressive, a timid dog is the most likely to attack.

I gulp as I crouch, nerves knotting my stomach.

Shauna and I got evicted from multiple homes due to my need to rescue strays I found in the streets. At times, it seemed like they found me. Never has an animal not warmed in my presence and learned to trust me. I ignore my rolling stomach.

He is large for a dog, bigger than a German Shepherd, but smaller than a Bernese Mountain dog. His specific breed is unknown to me.

At two feet away, he stiffens, looking over my shoulder at Marcus. He drops lower to the ground, a small snarl rippling from the side of his mouth.

I pause with my hand hovering in front of me.

His eyes narrow, and he bolts to the left. Straight into the street.

I gasp, standing to chase after him, as a pit forms in my stomach at all the cars. Before I take a step, a screeching sound fills my head. My hands grasp my temples, fingers digging into my scalp, as the sound grows. Through blurry vision, I watch the dog race between cars as the drivers slam on their breaks. My knees strike the concrete sidewalk as a crash echoes in the background.

Not again. Not again. Not again. Tears burn my eyes as pain ricochets through my skull. It has been two years since my last episode. Two years since I heard this sound, since my curse has reared its ugly head. Breathing shakily, I will myself not to lose my breakfast in public.

Within minutes, I hear sirens, but I have yet to uncurl from the ground. A thudding in my brain replaces the high-pitched scream. The stench of burnt tires assaults my nose. I look up, unveiling the commotion.

A three car pile-up blocks the road. Smoke rises from the car in the back, a fender bender for the truck in the front. But the sedan in the middle, if you could even call it one, now resembles an accordion. Nothing more than a twisted piece of metal with the windows blown out. The car is angled so I can't see anything, but there is no way the passenger, or passengers, could've survived.

"Are you okay?" Marcus's large hand holds my shoulder while he helps me into a sitting position.

I nod, unable to form words.

Marcus's focus jumps between me and the crash. The worry in his eyes makes it apparent he's unsure which to choose.

"Go," I croak.

His forehead crinkles. "Are you sure?"

"Yes, go help them."

He doesn't hesitate to walk away, already directing people to call 911 and explaining he's an emergency responder.

Heaving to my feet, I turn away from the commotion and my college campus. While I walk away, my teeth grind together to stifle the pain from my throbbing head.

TWO

Shauna barges into my room. "What're you doing in bed?"

I wince at the sound. My sister has always been a bull in a china shop, but the dull pound in my head makes it worse.

She pauses when she sees my face. "Are you okay? Are you sick?" Sitting on the side of my bed, she rubs my shoulder as she stares at me with worried eyes.

"It happened again," I mumble.

"What happened again? Did you get food poisoning? I told you all the coffee you consume was bound to hurt your stomach."

"No. *It* happened again." I frown as her eyes grow big in realization.

"What? But the doctor said you'd grow out of it. It's been years." Shauna brings her fingers to her mouth, chewing on her thumbnail. A bad habit she hasn't done in years.

"You mean I'd grow out of the thing the doctors couldn't diagnose?" Tears spring to my eyes. "I'm cursed," I whimper, throwing my arm over my eyes to hide my pain.

"Cara Maeve Winters, you are not cursed."

"But… it happened again." I say into the crook of my arm, muffling my words.

Shauna pulls at my wrist until my arm slides across to free my face. "Oh hush, you're overreacting. Does your head still hurt?"

My lip juts out. "Not as much. I took migraine pills and fell asleep. I woke an hour ago, and the pain is better."

"Then what're you still doing in bed?" She folds her arms across her chest. Her determination and goal oriented self would've been a much better choice to pursue a college degree.

"What?" I shoot her a wide-eyed stare. Why was my sister being so cruel? Granted, she never fully believed in my curse, but it's unlike her to be this cold.

"We're going out tonight. I already told you this." She stands and quirks an eyebrow at me as though she's waiting for me to bound out of bed after her.

"I'm not in the mood." I deflate further into my bed. If only I can sink in far enough I'll never have to leave it again. I can stay where it's safe, away from the world.

"Stop being a drama queen." Shauna's green eyes flash in determination.

"Shaun… someone died. Again," I utter. I thought I was finally free of this, but death was determined to follow me everywhere.

Her arms drop, her mouth opening a hair, before shaking her head to refocus. "Nope. It's a coincidence. Get up." She reaches forward and grabs my arm to drag me.

My brows furrow. "Coincidence?" I pry myself from her grasp. "Seriously, Shauna, this isn't a joke."

She's being unapologetically harsh. My sister has had to toe the line between friend, sister, and parent through our lives, and morphing between the roles can muddy our relationship at times. She will always be my favorite person in the world, but now was not the time to take an annoying big sister approach.

This isn't a coincidence. It wasn't in the past, and it isn't now. It's a curse. One which caused me to stop socializing and become distant from everyone until my only companions left were animals and my sister.

Her face drops, and her body crumples onto the mattress until she wraps me in her arms. "I'm sorry, okay? I'm surprised. It's been so long since this has happened. I forgot how to act." She pulls away. "But you should not let this define your life. It already has, and just last night you were complaining about needing a life. Don't let this control you. You are in charge of your life."

I am in charge of my own life.

Unease coils through my stomach. This doesn't feel true, and yet, a sliver of hope glistens in the back of my mind, making me want to believe it.

With a nod, I swing my legs over the side and leave the comfort of my warm bed. The cool floor against my bare feet refreshes me.

Shauna beams at me. "Okay, first, food. I brought home tacos. As your sister, I'll teach you to drink responsibly, and you should never drink on an empty stomach." She nods as though agreeing with herself.

"Aye-aye, captain," I salute her, putting on a fake persona which we both ignore as light laughter falls from us.

Fake it until you make it, right? I can do this. I can be like any young adult, go out and have fun without fearing the world. I have to do this.

"Come on. Let's hop to it!"

"Hold still for one more second," Shauna says as she prods at my eyelid with a brush.

"I told you to go with a natural look. This doesn't feel like it's natural," I whine.

"Just drink."

I stare at the fruity concoction Shauna made me, something she begrudgingly did after mocking me for gagging when I took a sip of a vodka shot. The drink is dangerously delicious, and I'm already halfway done with a small buzz. I need to eat another taco before leaving the house.

My eyes snag on the dark green bustier my sister wrangled me into earlier. The tight black pants and heeled boots were easier to convince me of, but the top hinges on lingerie and the nerves sloshes the liquid in my stomach.

"Why'd you make me wear this top?" I groan, bringing the straw of my drink to my lips. The liquid courage should be kicking in soon.

"Because it brings out your eyes," she mumbles over the tip of the blush brush sticking between her teeth.

"My poop green eyes? Great…"

Shauna steps back and glares at me, ripping the brush from her mouth. "They're marsh green, not poop green. Stop being self-deprecating, and own what the world gave you."

"I wish it'd given me your eyes," I grumble to myself.

My sister ignores my comment and leans down with an eyebrow pencil in hand. After a few seconds, she snaps back up. "Okay, all done!"

I rise from our dining room chair and waltz into my bedroom, where a full-length mirror hangs beside the door. With the smokey eyeshadow, light wings of eyeliner, and mascara, my eyes pop. The brown tints I hate about my green eyes are lighter. My jet black hair, which is flat as a board, hangs loosely to my belly button. No hair product or technology could bring volume to my straight hair, but at least it's got length. Despite cutting my hair to right below my shoulder each year, it reaches the top of my butt within months.

I don't recognize the petite body before me. The outfit gives the illusion of curves I don't have. For once I don't completely look like a twelve-year-old before puberty.

I spent most of my life underweight and sick. The smallest kid in every class. I was tested for anemia and various diseases multiple times, but everything would come back negative. Only in the last two years I have put on weight, thank you nutrition drinks meant for children, and got rid of my sickly look. However, I still desire to put on more muscle to turn my slight frame into something leaner, thus my failed attempt at exercise this morning.

"You outdid yourself, Shaun," I beam.

"You like it?" She squeals as she pops her head into my room. Her eyes sparkle as she takes in my full wardrobe. "You're a bombshell."

"Bombshell?" I chuckle. "I don't think people say that anymore." I shake my head, my hair falling across my face to cover the smirk on my lips.

"Doesn't matter what people say, it's still true."

I follow Shauna towards the front door of our shared apartment and reach for a taco sitting on the kitchen counter.

She slaps my hand away. "No way! You'll ruin my makeup." She ignores my pout and pulls me with one hand while using her other to order a ride share. "Don't drink and drive kids," she winks at me over her shoulder.

I roll my eyes. "This was your idea."

"I know, and I told you I would teach you how to have fun safely. That's rule number one." She closes the front door, and we cross the short, drabby hallway to the stairs.

"Shouldn't 'you must be of legal drinking age' be rule number one?"

"Don't be such a Debbie Downer. You drink the least out of anyone your age. You had one drink and I see you wobbling."

I glare at the back of her head before looking at my white knuckled grip on the handrail as we climb down from the third story. I sway a little from the mixture of the heels, alcohol, and tiny steps. I bristle over the fact my sister took notice before I did. Damn, alcohol. "Well, you made the single drink strong. It was more like three drinks in one."

"I, also, made it delicious," a wolfish grin spreads across her face as turns at the landing to the last flight of stairs. "I guess it's a good thing you ate." At the bottom, she waltzes to the front door, which has zero security, and throws the glass door open.

I scurry after her, ignoring the flip-flop of my gut as I step outside our building into the real world. I'm more of a jeans and t-shirt from secondhand shops kind of girl. This legitimately might be the fanciest I've ever looked in public. The exposure of the top half of my body doesn't help either.

Shauna strides over to a hybrid car waiting for us at the curb.

I follow with my eyes trained on the ground, ignoring the curious glances of strangers as they walk by. I pretend I'm in my normal clothes. Nothing weird here, everyone. People have worn crazier outfits in public. Although, they are probably wondering if they should call the cops because I look like a thirteen year old. With the makeup and outfit, maybe I could get away with fifteen.

Ducking my head, I slip into the backseat beside Shauna.

"Thanks," I call to the driver before shutting the door.
Shauna walks straight to the bouncer, ignoring the line in the alley.
Without any signs hanging, this is the only clue there is an entrance to
a club.

I raise my eyebrow at her. This girl oozes confidence. I wonder if
this is a trait passed onto her from our parents, but managed to skip
me. Or, maybe, it was something she had to learn from growing up
way too fast and way too young.

The bouncer gives my sister a nod before unlocking the barricade
to let us through. He doesn't give me a second glance. Clasping the
rope back in place, I hear his gruff voice ask for an ID from the next
person in line.

Bass reverberates through my body as we step through the black
door. The air is humid and smells of sweat and alcohol. Flashing
lights draw our path down a short hallway until it opens to a large
dance floor. A churning mass of bodies dances while laser lights
pierce the space. The disjunction makes the smooth dancing choppy.

"I need a drink," Shauna shouts into my ear over the music.

I nod to her and mouth *I'll follow*. There is no way I am leaving her
side.

My body shakes with adrenaline, and not the good kind. Is there a
way butterflies can metamorphose into something bigger? Like bats?
Because these are not gentle little bugs flapping around in my
stomach and making me want to dissolve into a dark corner. How
did Shauna convince me to do this again?

Shauna leans on the bar to give the male bartender her drink order. He flashes her a smile, giving her a once over with his eyes. She ignores his obvious interest. Poor guy doesn't realize he has no chance.

As I watch my sister evade the bartender's charm, a hand grips my waist and pulls me back. I freeze. Slowly, I turn my head to peer over my right shoulder.

A guy with dark blonde hair and five o'clock shadow gives me a lazy smile. His droopy eyes show his inebriation, which is confirmed when his whiskey breath fumes across my face.

"Hey, wanna dance?" He leans forward, using me to support his weight.

My ankle wobbles from the strain. I shake my head.

He ignores my unease and decline, grinding against my backside to the beat of the music.

I blanche and my mind blanks. How do I get out of this situation?

"Watch it, buddy. She's with me."

THREE

My sister shoves the man away, causing his hand to slip off my waist. Shauna flings her arm over my shoulders as she puts a drink in my hand.

I fumble, grasping it with both hands, as the syrupy liquid spills on my knuckles.

"Drink up, darling. We gotta hit the dance floor soon." Shauna smirks.

The guy takes a step towards us but stops in his tracks when my sister whips her head towards him with a glare. "Beat it."

With a huff, the guy turns and stalks off into the crowd. As soon as he is out of sight, Shauna drops her arm. "Seems there are creeps no matter where you go."

I attempt to hand her drink back, but she shakes her head and grabs a second one off the bar. She raises it in a toast to me before knocking it back. The light pink liquid in my glass ripples from the bass of the song. I'm unsure what it was, but before I can second guess myself, I toss back the liquor. It burns down my throat and settles in my belly. My face screws tight at the sharp taste; I don't understand how people like this stuff.

Shauna snatches the empty glass from my hand, drops it on the edge of the bar, and turns towards the dance floor.

I hustle after her, like a baby duck following its mother, fearful another guy will bother me without her there.

We shove our way through the sweating bodies moving to the beat. Once in the center of the crowd, my sister turns and starts swaying her hips. I eye her warily, standing stock still amongst everyone.

Shauna tilts her head back and laughs, but I can't hear her. She grabs my hands and pulls them one at a time to help loosen me up. All I need to do is step on her feet and I'd seem like a five year old dancing with an adult.

I burst into a fit of giggles at how ridiculous we look.

A wide grin forms across her face as I start to move on my own. Releasing my hands once more, she throws her own above her head as the beat drops.

I lean my head back, swaying it from side to side. My hair swishes against my shoulder blades, and I close my eyes, allowing the music to encompass my senses. The bass beats through my body. Tingles course through me from the mixture of alcohol and music. I smile to myself from the feel.

The DJ transitions into the next song, and everyone cheers as they jump. Lyrics I don't know mix in, and everyone in the crowd sings along, including Shauna.

Her eyes hook onto the female performer on stage, and a smile tugs at her lips.

My eyes flutter shut as the beat continues to rock through me. This isn't my usual music, but in person I can see the appeal. I move in time with those around me— jumping, grinding, and swaying to the variations within the melodies.

Soon I hold my hair in a ponytail off my neck as sweat beads down my skin. I should have brought a hair tie. With my sister's short hair, it's not something she would've thought of and my hair feels like a shield against my barely-there top.

Both of us lose ourselves to our own worlds. This time no one bothers me, thankfully. From the heat on my back, multiple bodies have stepped close to me, but within seconds they move away. I assume Shauna is the reason for this. If looks could kill, she'd be an assassin.

The music switches to top hits, no longer having the same lull of electronic music being mixed live for us, but it still has the perfect beat to dance to.

"I'm going to go say hi to my friend," Shauna leans to shout to me. Her eyes catch on the DJ as she leaves the stage.

I give her a thumbs up in encouragement.

"I won't be far. I promise." Her face scrunches in worry.

I wave her off as I continue to dance. No one has tried to dance with me in a while. I'm certain everyone understands not to bother me by this point. Plus, the alcohol and music has loosened me enough to where, for once, my mind feels free.

With a nod, she walks into the crowd and disappears.

My body continues to move as though it has a mind of its own. Five songs later, despite my momentary confidence, my stomach squirms. Perhaps it's the alcohol, or the heat. There's a good chance it's dehydration.

The hairs on the back of my neck stand on end. I turn to see if someone is behind me.

People grinding against each other assault my eyes. No one is there, but I can't rid the feeling of someone watching me. The need for space and fresh air consumes my mind. I push my way through the crowd towards a side exit. I'll find Shauna after I take a breather.

Shoving open the door, crisp air hits my face, the droplets of sweat turning cool against my skin. An overhead light brightens half the alley, which is the opposite side of the building from the entrance. Here trash cans loiter around the space instead of people.

I lean against the brick wall and close my eyes, allowing a deep breath to calm my body. A slight buzz rings in the back of my mind. I'm unsure if it is leftover effects from earlier today, the booze, or the loud music. My lungs fill with the cool air, but it's cut short when a glass bottle skimming across the ground echoes in the depths of the alleyway.

My body stiffens.

I turn my head toward the sound and lean away from the wall to peer into the shadows. "Is anyone there?"

Silence greets me.

The hair on my arms stand on end as goosebumps sweep across my skin. I listen, holding my breath, but the only penetrating sound is my racing heart.

I think it's time I find Shauna.

A small whimper escapes the darkness.

I startle at the sound of an animal in pain. I take hesitant steps further into the alley, and reach into my back pocket to pull out my cell phone. I press a button on the screen and the flashlight feature helps guide me.

A discarded fast food bag, empty soda cans, piled cardboard boxes, and endless beer bottles litter the ground.

Another whine slips to my ears.

It's coming from behind a large trash bin to my right.

I tiptoe forward, avoiding the broken glass, and when I wind around the corner, I'm met with black fur curled in a ball.

A large head lifts, its pink tongue slipping back into its mouth from where it had been licking its back hind leg. Its muzzle sneers and it greets me with a growl.

It's the same dog from earlier today.

The wounded animal emits another grizzly sound, a warning sign I ignore as I push my phone forward to brighten the hind leg. A thick liquid matts the coat and based on the red paw prints I see on the ground, I assume it's blood.

"Hey, bud, I'm here to help." I take a tentative step, but halt when the dog rumbles. I lower myself toward the ground. "I promise I won't hurt you."

His eyes dart over my shoulder, and with a show of fangs, he snarls.

A hand lands on my shoulder, causing me to jolt. There's a moment where I wonder if it's my sister before the scent of a distillery wafts over me.

"Need help?" A gruff voice asks.

I huff in relief as I turn. "Actually, yes, this dog is hurt and—" I take in the man's face from the bar, the same one who had gotten a little too friendly.

He drops his hand as I stand to face him, but he doesn't step away.

A leering smirk fills his dark face. "I meant do *you* need help," he says as he takes a step closer.

The dog growls, causing the man to stop, but cuts off with a small whine.

My eyes flit over my shoulder to see the dog has attempted to stand.

The guy glares down at the dog. "Get out of here, mutt." He raises the beer bottle, and lobs it to the right of me. It smashes against the brick wall, causing shards of glass to rain down over the helpless animal.

"Back off!" I say as I shove him away.

The man scoffs. "You're going to protect some rabies infected stray?" He throws his head back and cackles. Without any grace, he barrels forward, and my small stature isn't enough to stop him as he knocks me aside. He bends over the snarling dog. "Damn cock blocking flea bag," he spits before standing and lodging his boot into the dog's side.

The dog yelps as it crashes against the wall, landing onto the broken glass.

Rage fills my mind, blocking all reason.

Who does this man think he is, hurting an innocent animal?

Before I can think twice, I am off the ground and leap onto the man's back. I grab his dark blonde hair, giving it a yank back until he howls in pain, stumbling backwards from my forceful pull. His heel catches, and the ground rushes towards me as we both fall backwards.

A sharp crack hits my elbow. The air escapes my lungs with a wheeze when the guy lands on top of me. I suck in gasps of air. My head rings. I wrap my legs around the man's waist and hold his hair firm in my grasp. I blink away the tears from my eyes.

To my left, the dog stands a couple of feet away. Its dark golden eyes are torn as they look between me, the man I hold in a death grip, and the opening to the alley. It takes another step towards me.

"Go! Get out of here!" I yell.

The dog hesitates.

"Go!" A shrill sound escapes my throat.

The dog jumps before tucking its tail and half limping, half running away. At the end of the alley, it looks back once before rounding the corner.

The man reaches up and pries my hand off.

A gasp escapes my lips from the pain in my fingers.

He drops my hand, and uses the freedom to push himself off the ground.

My legs lose their grip and I slip off his back, landing back on the ground with my black hair lying across my face and skewing my vision.

"If you want to lock those legs around me, baby, I have a much more fun way." The man grips my hair and pulls me to my feet.

I have no choice but to follow to help lessen the pain in my scalp. I bite back a cry.

He backs me up until my shoulders press against the chilled brick wall. He leans towards me, licking his lips with malicious intent in his eyes.

My heart pounds as my arms cross in front of me. I brace them against his chest to keep a few inches of distance between us.

He presses himself further against me and I grit my teeth as weakness tugs at my muscles.

Damnit, I really need to start working out.

The tugging on my hair intensifies. My head tilts back with a whimper.

His gaze locks onto mine. His blue eyes are predatory. He glances at my shaking arms trying to block him. Excitement flashes across his wretched features at my distress. His sour breath fumes over my face.

My stomach churns. I won't be able to hold on much longer. Tears sting the back of my eyes as my heartbeat quickens. A ringing sounds through my head. With no options, I take in a deep breath and scream at the top of my lungs.

The man drops me.

I slump onto the ground. My abdomen contracts while I continue to scream.

He covers his ears as he doubles over in pain. His face is red, and eyes squeeze shut.

Please let someone hear me.

The man lands on his knees.

By the time my air runs out, a third figure stands in the alley.

Whisper of Darkness is Available Now

About the Author

Characters and their worlds have inundated Kristen's mind since she was a kid. Traveling to far off places and having words on a piece of paper transform into entire scenes pulling at her emotions is an obsession.

Her goal as a fantasy author isn't solely to relish in her imagination, but to bring representation to this genre. She wants stories with characters who are diverse inside and out. Their differences are not the focal point of the narrative, but rather a natural part of their being. Due to this, you will often not only find characters of varying ethnicities, but also of the LGBTQ+ community, who battle diseases, are neurodiverse, and plenty of other areas that make us all so different from each other. These are not their defining qualities. It's simply a part of who they are.

When Kristen isn't cooped up on her computer or curled up with a book, she is often outdoors-- traveling, hiking, snorkeling, diving, camping, etc.

Currently, she resides in California with her husband and fur babies (two dogs and a cat).